Gerry Anderson's

INTO INFINITY
PLANETFALL

The crew of the Altares (L-R): Katharine Levy *as Jane Masters,* Brian Blessed *as Tom Bowen,* Nick Tate *as Captain Harry Masters,* Joanna Dunham *as Anna Bowen, and* Martin Lev *as David Bowen.*

Gerry Anderson's

INTO INFINITY
PLANETFALL

A Novel by
Gregory L. Norris

ANDERSON
ENTERTAINMENT

Gerry Anderson's
INTO INFINITY
PLANETFALL

First published in Great Britain by Anderson Entertainment Ltd., 2019

INTO INFINITY/PLANETFALL novel copyright © 2019
by Gregory L. Norris
THE DAY AFTER TOMORROW/INTO INFINITY copyright © 1975 and
2019 by Anderson Entertainment Ltd.
Frontispiece photo © 1975 and 2019 by Anderson Entertainment Ltd.

The moral rights of the author have been asserted.

All characters in this publication are fictitious and any resemblance to real
persons, living or dead, is purely coincidental.

All rights reserved.
No part of this publication may be reproduced, stored in a retrieval
system, or transmitted, in any form or by any means, without the prior
permission in writing of the publisher, nor be otherwise circulated in any
form of binding or cover other than that in which it is published and
without a similar condition including this condition being imposed on the
subsequent purchaser.

ISBN **978-1727367430**

Editor: Robert E. Wood
Cover Design: Martin Jones / martipants.co.uk

Anderson
Entertainment Ltd.
Hornbeam House,
Bidwell Road
Norwich, NR13 6PT

www.anderson-entertainment.co.uk

For Ed Bishop, Derek Wadsworth, Don Fellows, and Ernest George Hatem III, fellow travelers and explorers of the great, unknown universe.

Chapter One

It was happening again.

The Space Authority light ship *Altares* was coming apart after arrowing straight into the maw of the black hole. Streamers of fantastic color lit at the direct vision space windows and portholes, bathing the interior of the ship in a kaleidoscopic effulgence. The glow from their universe chased them down into the whirlpool, it, too, unable to escape the singularity's hunger.

At first, she'd attempted to hold their course steady. As the ship's copilot, it was Jane Masters' duty, and a commitment she would honor to the end, if indeed this was an ending for *Altares* and her crew of five. It certainly looked to be. Thunder pulsed at Jane's ears and smothered her shouts to the others. One moment, she was still seated in the second of the two pilot chairs facing the forward space window, the navigation controls bucking against her grip, and the violent unknown before them. *Altares* was a solid ship, laid out from stem to stern in the shape of a metal arrow. The next second, she was evicted from her chair, and the arrow was tumbling out of control.

What followed was a dance between the light ship's compartments – Flight Deck to Navigation, and from there back and forth through the Monitoring Area and Crew's Quarters to the dead end where the Photon Drive unit was housed. Oh, there was more to *Altares*, much more beyond the core star-drive that had gotten them so deep into the heart of their former galaxy, and was now leading them to their deaths. Past the Photon Drive were the enormous tanks filled with the chemicals used to fuel the light ship's standard-speed engines; above their heads, the massive directional antenna that housed transmitters, particle scoop, and *Altares*' powerful forward laser cannon, designed to clear space debris from the way ahead. Below, the ship's dual wings, home to stabilizers, energy transfer units, and the hangars containing a pair of EVA support craft Jane had nicknamed 'Kites' for their whimsical design, which reminded her of a painting her late mother had created on a planet, during a life, untold light years at their backs.

Altares was a sturdy ship. The sturdiest. But Jane was convinced their only home was doomed to be crushed or come apart under the unholy stress being forced upon her hull. Reality blurred. For a terrifying instant, she suffered double vision. There were two Janes, and two of everyone else—Anna Bowen, their Chief Medical Officer; two Tom Bowens, ship's navigator; two David Bowens, Tom and Anna's young son; and two Harry Masters. Jane's father—*Altares'* pilot and captain of the mission—receded from her outstretched hand. She was falling farther away from him. At the porthole, she spied a second *Altares*, flying in formation beside them. Not only was the black hole readying to obliterate them, it was determined to duplicate their pain so that the end would be twice as agonizing.

Two crews. Two *Altares*. She remembered thinking in that final moment how the forces inside a singularity could warp time as well as space. And she remembered thinking, *there goes an alternate version of us, a parallel timeline.* Then the second *Altares* vanished, and the light grew blinding as the savage shaking gradually stilled.

"Some say that if you go through a rotating black hole, you'll end up in another universe," Anna had said after they got trapped in the singularity's gravitational pull. "Or even a new dimension. We don't know. But if we do survive it, there's no way back."

They *had* survived it, thought Jane. So why was *Altares* shaking again, coming apart at the seams?

Something's not right, her inner voice

reasoned. *Something's...*

Jane opened her eyes. The familiar outline of her sleeping bunk pulled free of the kaleidoscope. She was in the Crew's Quarters, where she'd gone to rest following the *Altares'* successful emergence out of the black hole. They hadn't been crushed or shaken apart, as she'd feared. So why was the light ship trembling around her?

She sat up and reached for the white jacket and boots that completed her powder blue regulation uniform ensemble. *Altares* quivered. Blinking the last of the sleep from her eyes, Jane headed through the throat of the light ship's top deck, holding onto the lengths of metal safety rail as she advanced into the empty Monitoring Area. For a terrible moment, the thought that she alone had survived the singularity fueled her growing worry that the others had vanished onto that alternate *Altares* glimpsed briefly through the porthole.

Then, in the Navigation Area, the most reassuring sight greeted her. Two figures manned the navigation table, father and son clad in fawn and chocolate uniforms with white jackets and boots.

"Keep her steady, Skipper," said Tom Bowen. "A little more's all we need."

"Another three hundred meters should suffice," David Bowen called above the chop.

"Three hundred, confirmed," said Anna. She stood at the wall of computers that lined part of the Navigation Area.

Jane shot a look toward the direct vision porthole across from the chart table, alerted by a flash of light. The kaleidoscopic deluge sucked into the black hole's maw with them was back. They had returned to her nightmare, only Jane was awake.

"Dad?" Jane called.

Anna turned and spoke Jane's name. Then their doctor hastened across the Navigation Area and guided Jane over to the nearest vacant chair.

"What's happening?" Jane asked.

"We should be there in a few seconds, Jane," Anna said.

"Three hundred meters down, confirmed," David barked. "Initiate scans and extend the particle scoop."

Altares jolted and groaned around them. Her heart still in a gallop, Jane again turned toward the porthole. A fireball streaked past, the color robust against a palette of mostly blue.

"Particle scoop extended," Harry Masters answered from the Flight Deck.

"Anna-!" This came from Bowen.

Anna maneuvered back to the wall of computers. "Initiating scan."

Jane stood, drawn to the porthole. Beyond the circle of reinforced glass, a stunning image spread before her eyes: wispy clouds, blue skies above, the firmament of an alien world's surface far below. Another fireball blew past, and now she understood its source was one of the light ship's steering rockets.

The *Altares* was cutting through atmosphere.

"We've got it, Harry," Anna announced. "You can take her back up!"

"Thank God for that," her father answered. "Hold tight, folks. Ascending back into orbital pattern."

The steering rockets fired again. Gravity pulled on Jane's insides. The heaviness deepened before it loosened its grip. Shadows fell over the porthole. When Jane looked again, they were high over the blue planet and once more in orbit.

They gathered around the chart table. Anna passed the printout to Harry Masters, who gave it a quick scan before handing it to Bowen.

David read the results. "By volume, the planet's atmosphere contains 78.09 percent nitrogen, 20.95 percent oxygen, .93 percent argon, and 0.04 percent carbon dioxide. The rest is mostly water vapor."

"Which makes it a wonderful discovery," Anna said. "An Earth-like planet perfectly positioned in its yellow dwarf star's circumstellar habitable zone."

"Brilliant," Masters said. "Only that's not exactly what we took *Altares* down into the atmosphere to determine."

She'd wanted to chastise her father for letting her sleep—Jane was ship's copilot, and being in that chair beside him was more important than rest, no matter how much she needed it. But her father's expression stopped Jane from complaining.

"Hydrogen," she said.

Masters nodded. "Or a lack thereof. Like on Earth, there's an absence of hydrogen gas in this planet's atmosphere."

"If hydrogen molecules bounce up, traveling at an escape velocity of eleven-point-three kilometers per second, they leave the atmosphere and don't return," said Anna.

"Which leaves us with a serious problem," Bowen sighed.

Masters nodded. "If we don't replenish our chemical fuel supply soon, *Altares'* tanks are going to run empty, and we'll be dead up here in orbit."

Chapter Two

She was constructed in orbit topside of Space Station Delta, and hadn't been designed to navigate a planet's atmosphere. Then again, David mused, *Altares* hadn't been envisioned to fly straight down into a rotating black hole, but on both accounts the light ship had outperformed expectations.

The blue planet rolled far beneath them, its cracked terrain, water bodies, and crimson-tinged impact craters visible beyond the Navigation Area's porthole. The view distracted him from his work. Following their brazen plunge down into the new planet's stratosphere in search of hydrogen gas, the second ship-wide diagnostic in as many days was underway. *Altares* had fared well following her arrival to this reality, suffering only minor damage, all things considered. Her charge through the planet's upper atmosphere had resulted in even less thus far, according to their central computer—a power fluctuation in Subcompartment D.

Harry Masters exited the Flight Deck. "Anything else, David?"

David turned from the stunning panorama of the blue planet beneath constellations of crystal-facet silver stars, the latter all floating among plumes of gauzy purple gas. "So far, Captain, it's just the forward laser cannon and that nagging energy drain in Subcompartment D. The rest of *Altares* is running like she was still docked atop Space Station Delta."

Masters smiled. "Good work. Tom?"

Bowen glanced up from the chart table. "Skipper, apart from an asteroid field that could be planetary remains or debris ejected out of the singularity, that shiny blue sphere beneath us is the only world in this system. No convenient gas giants out there for us to pop in and refuel at, I'm afraid."

The smile dropped from Masters' face. "Damn."

"Don't write us off just yet," Bowen continued. He waved Masters over to the chart table, whose view screen displayed the singularity at their backs.

On this side of space, the singularity was a white hole, an exit point whose event horizon was marked by the particles of light being swallowed down the black hole's throat. Bowen adjusted the picture. New coordinates turned the light ship's external cameras two degrees toward the purple gas clouds that magnified the silver light cast from the nearest stars.

"I believe we've found the closest refueling depot," Bowen said.

The chart table's gauges tracked the distance — a sizeable gulf separated them from the closest plume.

"That means—" Masters started.

"I know. Activating the Photon Drive before we've had the chance to do a complete systems evaluation. For all we know, the same problems that got us here could repeat. But as I see it, we don't have much of a choice."

Masters nodded. "When do we depart?"

"I'd suggest in twelve hours, Skipper. Time enough for us to get that forward laser cannon repaired, and resolve whatever's going on down there in the lower deck."

Masters rested both hands on David's shoulders. "And for some of us to get rested."

"I'm not tired," David said, which wasn't exactly the truth.

"No doubt, but I'd like the entire crew alert, and you're already two hours past your scheduled break."

David looked at his father, who, despite his smile, tipped his chin in the direction of the Crew's Quarters. "You heard our captain. Besides, the exploration of the planet's been postponed for now. Go on."

David headed toward the arch between compartments. There, he turned back. "We are going down there, aren't we?"

Masters nodded. "Once *Altares* is full up, you just try to stop us making planetfall and taking a look around."

David smiled. "Good night."

Masters flashed the boy a thumbs-up.

"Good night, son," his father said.

They hadn't brought much aboard with them, one holdall each. David's had contained several new decks of playing cards, though he had yet to open one. Mostly, he brought books with him. Despite the light ship's reference library containing more truths and fictions than could possibly be read over the course of an entire lifetime, he preferred physical, printed volumes.

From beneath his pillow, David drew out the battered paperback copy of Robert Louis Stevenson's *Treasure Island*. He was only a few pages into Part 1—"The Old Buccaneer". Jim Hawkins, Trelawney, and Doctor Livesey had yet to board the *Hispaniola* in search of Captain Flint's buried treasure. He'd read the book twice before—the first time during their training for the *Altares* mission. Still, how he loved his fictional predecessor's adventure, and lost himself in the words until, a few pages later, sleep claimed him.

Masters opened the locker, which contained five atmosuits and an equal number of helmets. Two of the suits were pale blue, the remaining three two-tone, fawn and chocolate. He had no trouble identifying which atmosuit was his.

"While I'm out there," Masters said.

Anna lifted the helmet. "I'll try to resolve that power fluctuation down here."

Masters stepped into the atmosuit and secured magnetic seals. He took the helmet from Anna and donned it, then secured the final lock. Once the suit's sensors detected everything was in place, the suit activated. Masters tapped the helmet's radio. The horn activated, patching him into the ship's intercom.

"Jane, hold her steady."

"Yes, Captain," Jane answered.

Anna signaled he was set to go with a thumbs-up, and Masters approached the hatch, marked "1". The airlock, a perfect circle, split into quarters and opened when he stabbed the door controls. The dark landscape beyond lit. He plodded from *Altares* into the Kite's passenger section—a molded bench for four set beneath space windows and a storage compartment for transporting equipment.

Masters turned back. Anna handed him the repair kit and then the requisitioned replacement parts from storage. Masters secured the gear.

"Good luck, Harry," Anna said.

He nodded and closed the airlock. Anna backed away and faced the direction of Subcompartment D.

Masters took to the pilot's chair. After so much time in *Altares*' cockpit, the Kite's controls were a tight fit. He ignored his discomfort, did his best to forget that every second up here put them closer to running out of the chemical fuel that fed the ship's conventional engines and steering rockets, and completed his checklist.

"Opening things up, *Altares*," he spoke into the horn.

"Roger that, Kite 1," Jane answered.

Masters thumbed the button that rolled back the starboard hangar door. Light from the day face of the blue planet below flooded the Kite. In sequence, he started her up. The Kite also ran on the chemical mix and would be good to go for his needs. Magnetics disengaged. He gripped the steering column, nudged her down and out of the hangar, and exited beneath the *Altares*' starboard wing.

The majesty of his surroundings struck Masters in a way he hadn't known standing aboard the light ship, which was vaster in scope and less open to the surrounding universe. The blue planet appeared full and beautiful before the Kite's forward space window, as did those vibrant crystal stars in the distance.

Even more breathtaking was *Altares* herself after he boosted the Kite up past her starboard wing and toward her topside, passing the light ship's superstructure of hull armor, fuel tanks, and those few direct vision ports, beyond which the crew worked in service of the mission. Higher, parallel to the directional antenna that housed the forward laser cannon, he was reminded of the vessel's majesty, from the forward prow of her command module all the way back to the Photon Drive unit's propulsion vent.

Altares was beautiful.

The light ship had traveled far from her planet of origin. Her crew had accomplished their original mission to reach Alpha Centauri and launch the network of long-range communications satellites that would assist in future manned missions beyond Earth's solar system. They'd survived the malfunction in the Photon Drive caused by the capture of a superluminal particle that got scooped up and knocked around in the system, traveled an unknown number of light years off course, and navigated through the black hole.

The light ship looked great, considering the demands that had been made of her.

The first known planet exhibiting similar traits to Mother Earth rolled beneath them. Yes, by all reckoning the *Altares* mission had exceeded the original goals many times over.

Masters nudged the Kite closer to the antenna, extended the magnetic arm, and fixed the smaller ship in position. He cycled decompression, opened the hatch, and clamped his safety line secure. Then Harry Masters stepped out of the Kite, the first human being to set foot in this new, mysterious universe.

Chapter Three

Absent was the usual background noise Anna associated with their life one deck above her present location on *Altares*. The constant hum and sweep of scanners, the ping-pong melody of the electronic eyes keeping watch on surrounding space for incoming dangers, was replaced by a singular thrum that Anna's imagination translated into a giant's heartbeat. She supposed it was—the light ship's. On the slow amble down the barely-lit corridor to the hatch leading into Subcompartment D, her memory called up the ship's schematics. Arteries and the ship's metal skeleton converged here, near the core of *Altares*' power systems, which made the analogy of a pulse believable.

She'd been down here three times before—first during the official tour while the light ship was still anchored to Delta Station in orbit around the Earth. The second came after the last of their shakedown cruises through Earth's solar system, which had targeted Neptune during which the particle scoop had replenished the chemical fuel tanks through an atmospheric dive much like the maneuver they would soon attempt in the stellar gas plumes. Following Neptune, a power relay in the air purification system had stuck while the ship was still in the gas giant's outer layers performing the emergency-refueling maneuver. She'd corrected the malfunction.

And how Delta Station's commander, Jim Forbes, had praised her heroics.

Anna halted her advance and reached to the wall for support. She gripped the metal safety rail running up to the hatch leading into D.

"Maybe we should make you captain of the mission," Forbes said in her thoughts.

Anna closed her eyes, aware that breathing had become difficult. Jim Forbes materialized in her memory. For long days and across light years—an entire *universe*, in fact—she'd kept thoughts of him banished behind mental revetments. How his crisp white commander's uniform with its black collar and stripes along both arms fit his physique in a way that should have been criminal. The scent of his skin—clean, male sweat mixed with the brand of soap he used. How she'd almost opted to stay behind, on Delta, after their brief connection.

In the end, Anna chose David and her marriage to Tom over a life with Forbes. For the first time since *Altares* emerged from the black hole, it struck her that Forbes was gone, long dead according to Einstein's Time Dilation Theory. Time on Earth passed at a faster advance than their life lived on the light ship. And who knew how linear time had been affected during their crossing over to this new universe upon leaving their old?

Forbes, Space Station Delta, maybe even the very planet of their origin, were gone.

Tears stung at the corners of her eyes. Anna fought them, but failed. The first few slipped down her cheeks. Beyond the watery veil, ghosts from the past manifested—Forbes, along with that previous Anna Bowen.

"You performed admirably," he said, a blurry white phantom with black lines cutting through.

"Only because of your training," the ghost dressed in fawn and chocolate answered.

"You're being modest. I have half a mind to reassign you to Delta, keep you here and all to myself."

Silence followed that declaration, which was innocent enough on the surface, but on that day lost to the past, breathing hadn't been any easier, and the pressure in the air seemed to double at the bottommost point on *Altares*.

"Commander…"

"*Jim*, please. It's just you and me now,

Anna."

One ghost reached for the other. Anna closed her eyes in the present, stemming further tears. What had followed—Forbes reaching for her hand, the breathless pall before their kiss, the thrum of *Altares*' heart and the gallop of hers in counterpoint—continued, broadcast onto the insides of her eyelids.

Anna shook her head and wiped her eyes. After reaching Alpha Centauri and deploying the satellite chain, a message beamed from Earth contained his congratulations for having fulfilled their mission. It was the last time she heard his voice, and the sense of what she'd lost had pursued her deeper into the galaxy like an unwanted second shadow. How much distance needed to pass before she was fully over Jim Forbes?

The horn resting on her right ear chirped, shocking her back to the moment. Anna sucked in a deep, cleansing breath before reaching up to tap the activation button, opening the channel to the top deck.

"How are things down there?" her husband asked.

Apart from the ghosts that had faded back into the ether, Anna was alone. Even so, she forced herself to smile. "Just getting my bearings, Tom."

Bowen chuckled over the intercom, and how that sound reassured her. "I thought you knew every meter of this ship intimately?"

Some sections more intimately than others, she thought, resuming her approach to Subcompartment D's hatch.

"Just checking in to make sure that you're all right, sweetheart."

Her smile persisted, no longer forced. "Thanks for being there."

"Always. Navigation Area out."

The horn chirped again and then went silent. If memories of Jim Forbes were unwelcome, she was happy for this reminder that she'd made the proper decision. Anna jabbed her code into the keypad. The round airlock, identical to others around the ship, uncoupled into four pie wedges that drew back into the surrounding bulkhead. The area beyond sat in a darkness broken only by the barest flicker of power diodes. She activated the light controls. Overheads switched on in sequence, throwing the familiar white glow across a long, narrow corridor with power conduit running the length of one wall, with the junction—her destination—housed at the other.

She ducked through the hatch and moved into Subcompartment D. Forbes was gone. So was everything else that mattered, save what mattered most. David and Tom were directly above, and *Altares* was damaged and running low on fuel. She exorcized Jim Forbes from her focus and headed down the corridor.

Instantly, a frisson of disquiet struck her,

halting Anna several meters in. Tom had been correct in his statement about her knowledge of the light ship's layout from top to bottom, stem to stern. This was not the same Subcompartment D she'd traversed following the Neptune maneuver. The junction was where she expected, and the light glimmered over the access terminal, which jibed with the diagnosis of a power fluctuation—a minor sting considering all the light ship could have suffered between Earth and high orbit above the blue planet. Even so, a minor injury that needed tending. The toolkit hanging from a strap at her shoulder grew heavy as her confusion worsened.

No, the discrepancy was real, and located past the junction and a section of bulkhead running smoothly toward the aft of the compartment. That area of solid wall had been designated as overflow storage during the shakedown cruise to Neptune—an entire room of open space. She knew this to be a fact because that's where Forbes took her for their kiss.

Anna's gaze fixed on the solid length of wall, featureless apart from the same likeness to other metal cladding used throughout the rest of *Altares*. On the other side was a room, she was sure of it.

The exorcism hadn't been a success. Forbes was back, and she was with him.

"Do you know where we're standing?" he asked.

That past version of Anna glanced around

at the power conduit and featureless walls of the box-shaped empty compartment. "Overflow storage?"

"The future," Forbes said. Then all emotion ironed off his handsome face.

At the time, she'd assumed he was speaking about the greater scope of things. The future. *Altares*. While the Earth Authority struggled to fix the situation below, the Space Authority was constructing giant new stations in high orbit and readying to launch manned missions far beyond Sol. Her own future had seemed clear following Neptune—soon, she'd depart aboard *Altares* for Alpha Centauri. But the way ahead wasn't so certain following what happened next, when he took her hand, kissed it, and then crushed his mouth over hers.

No tears born of regret came this time. Anna's focus remained on the inconsistency—solid bulkhead where a room had existed.

She blinked herself out of the trance and hastened back to the junction. Anna relaxed her shoulder and set to work opening the panel. The light continued to tick on and off, signaling the problem. She traced the fluctuation to a power feed coupling. One of the lines had overloaded and tripped, putting the burden completely on its partner. An easy fix. She keyed in the sequence to redistribute evenly, flipped the unit back on to active, and the ticking light stabilized into a solid green.

Problem solved, thought Anna.

Unexpected movement teased the corner of her eye. She tensed, turned, and standing before her in the corridor of Subcompartment D was Jim Forbes. He was dressed in his crisp white Delta Station uniform with its black collar and sleeve stripes.

"Jim?" Anna gasped.

Forbes smiled. "This is all about second chances," he said.

Anna froze. Forbes, here? Impossible!

And as soon as that thought was made, the gods listened, and Jim Forbes vanished.

Chapter Four

Masters clipped his tether to the third lowest on the set of metal rungs running up the antenna. The laser's output coupler was shattered, the facets reminding him of broken mirror. *I hope this doesn't mean seven years of bad luck*, he thought, chuckling at the notion.

He fixed the toolkit to the nearest length of the ship's hull via its magnetic strip and got to work. The damage ran deeper than the output coupler. The entire plasma tube beyond the firing window had burned out. Luckily, his atmosuit held a full charge—enough for three hours—and he had replacement packs to ensure the job wouldn't be interrupted until it was complete. He set to work, removing the fractured components in order. On Space Station Delta, a team of specialists would have tackled a project of this scope. This far from Earth, there was only Harry Masters. Luckily, the weightlessness of space was on his side.

The enormous mirror detached. Harry eased it back down to the Kite. How easy it would be to send the useless debris flying off into space, where it was likely to float for the next few billion years until the system's sun burned up all of its hydrogen and, starving, committed solar suicide. But they were coming back to this world after a brief stop to refuel *Altares'* chemical engines, and best not to run into debris discarded in orbit.

Besides, that kind of thinking had led the mother planet to the tenebrous state it occupied when they'd departed. No, out here they were thinking in new ways. Best to modify behaviors as well.

The powerful laser's firing window detached without issue. Removing the shattered plasma tube didn't prove so easy. The cylinder held fast, resisting his best efforts to withdraw it from the assembly.

"She's stuck, Tom," Masters called into the horn. "Whatever did this fused the plasma tube in place."

Bowen answered, "Want me to suit up and join you, Skipper?"

Another set of hands would make the job easier, but he needed Bowen's eyes on those fuel levels, Jane's hands on the pilot controls, and David focused on the planetary data.

Groaning, Masters tugged again. "I'd like

you to, yes. But let's stick with the plan. I'm not ready to give up just yet."

There, working the laser's assembly, the question of what had happened again taunted him. According to the damage, their forward laser cannon appeared to have taken a direct hit from weapon's fire. The jagged black scar burned into the surrounding ship's armor would never get repaired; so far from home and a depot the size of Space Station Delta, the light ship would forever wear the scar as a badge of honor, albeit one cloaked in mystery.

Masters released the burned-out plasma tube. They'd used the forward laser as a test, firing it toward the gravitational source holding them in its grasp. The beam had distorted and was sucked down into what turned out being the black hole. To his knowledge, it hadn't fired again after that. Nor had the laser malfunctioned. So where did the damage come from?

His flesh prickled beneath the atmosuit's lining. Masters' lungs constricted. For a fraction of a second, his mind grasped at an image. There one instant, it was gone the next. He willed his lungs to fill up and redoubled his effort.

"Do you want to leave it, Harry? For after our return from those gas plumes?" Bowen asked.

"No, Tom. As it stands, I don't like us flying circles around that planet without a working forward laser cannon. We don't know what'll come at us out there in open space."

"Roger that, Skipper."

The broken unit shifted under his gloves. "I think I've got it. Just a little more..."

The damaged plasma tube detached in pieces. As he'd done with the useless output coupler and shattered firing window, Harry walked the segments back to the Kite, and then removed the replacement from its protective case. On his way back up the rungs, he paused. Beyond *Altares'* superstructure, the blue planet rolled in its orbit.

Magnificent, Masters agreed. At least fifty percent of the surface was covered in water, which lent it that familiar blue expression. The continent visible below his vantage point looked to be rocky desert, or perhaps an environment approximating Earth's savannahs. Even from this high up, the surface details were stunning, particularly the round impressions ringed in crimson that were likely impact craters.

Soon, once the light ship's immediate needs were resolved, they would travel down there and check out the lay of the land close up. Of course, exploring the blue planet would open them up to a new set of potential problems, the greatest of which would be whether or not to continue forward if the world beneath them turned out to be welcoming. Theirs was not a colonizing mission, but one of exploration and expanding human knowledge of space. Even the space of different universes.

Masters woke from the spell. He positioned the replacement plasma tube into the casing and was pleased by the reassuring snap as it fit the assembly, as designed. Then, he fixed the new firing window in place, and lastly secured the output coupler, completing repairs to the forward laser cannon.

"I'm coming in, *Altares*," he called into the horn. "Once I'm back aboard, we'll test the system."

"Understood, Skipper,' Bowen said.

Masters cast another look at the blue planet. If it was close enough to Earth-like to consider stopping for good and setting down new roots, they'd have that conversation. For now, *Altares*' mission was still in effect, and the light ship needed to be refueled.

He entered the Kite, demagnetized from the hull, and guided the smaller craft down and back into *Altares*' starboard hangar.

Anna greeted him at the airlock, and Masters instantly sensed that something was wrong. She looked shaken, worried.

"You okay?" he asked.

Anna shook her head. She hung up the atmosuit and handed Masters a bottle of water. He noted that she refused to make direct eye contact and reached for her as she turned toward the lift waiting to take them back up from the subcompartment to the top deck.

"Anna?"

She pulled against him, and Masters

released her. "I really need to get back to the Monitoring Area," was all the explanation she offered.

They rode the short distance in silence. The elevator glided to a stop, its doors opening on the rear of the Crew's Quarters. There, they parted company, Masters through to the Navigation Area, Anna to her domain in the light ship's medical compartment.

"Good work, Skipper," Bowen said.

He rose from the chart table and met Masters with a handshake.

In a lower voice, Masters asked, "Did anything happen while I was out there?"

Bowen's gaze drifted in the direction of the Monitoring Area. "No. Anna fixed the power fluctuation in Subcompartment D. With the forward laser cannon repaired, we should be operating at one hundred percent efficiency."

Masters forced a smile. "Good. Let's test that laser and then prepare to leave orbit."

Bowen nodded. Masters continued on through the arch and into the Flight Deck, where Jane manned the controls.

"How are we looking?"

"No problems, Dad. She's handling like a dream."

Masters climbed into the pilot's seat. "Good to know. What's the fuel situation?"

"Low. But we've got enough left in the tanks to get us moving toward those gas plumes. After that…"

"The Photon Drive," Masters said, and how that declaration tied his guts into knots.

She activated the bio-panel and stepped in front of it. The transparent medical scanner showed deep images of lungs, heart, and circulation. Of greater concern to Anna was the brain scan. Had she suffered a bleed? A trans-ischemic attack might explain why she was seeing phantoms. But the bio-panel found no evidence of TIA, and her chemistry came back as textbook normal. Apart from an elevated heartbeat, she was in perfect health.

And if that was true, so was the rest of it. She hadn't hallucinated seeing Jim Forbes below decks.

"Standby for test firing," David called over the intercom. "A five-second blast. Targeting now."

Anna ordered her heart to steady and marched out of the Monitoring Area for Navigation.

"Targeting systems locked along Orbital Reference Point one-one-eight," Masters said. "Fire."

Altares trembled as the forward laser cannon discharged its powerful green beam at open space. The porthole briefly lit. The flare waned.

"Again, just to be safe," Masters said. "Fire!"

The cannon erupted a second time, along the same path away from the planet and toward deep space.

"It looks like we're ready to go," said David.

Bowen added, "I'll say so."

Anna joined her husband and son at the chart table. "Tom, can you call up ship's specs and send them through to me in the Monitoring Area?"

"We're getting ready to break orbit, Anna. Can it wait?"

"Please, it's important."

Their eyes met. Bowen nodded and tapped at the chart table's controls. The view of the blue planet vanished, replaced by diagrams of *Altares*.

"I'm sending them through now, Anna."

She flashed a smile and returned to the Monitoring Area. There, she accessed the charts on the largest of the compartment's computer screens. To her dismay, the section of Subcompartment D she knew had been open storage, scene of her forbidden kiss with Forbes, showed only a length of solid wall.

Chapter Five

They worked together, falling into the orderly pattern. While Masters ran through his pre-flight checklist, at his right Jane followed hers.

"Countdown now at—mark—five minutes," David Bowen called from Navigation. "Countdown continues."

Masters cast a glance at the screen running over his and Jane's stations. "Activate navigation controls."

Tom Bowen moved from his seat at the chart table over to the wall of instruments running at his right. The computer terminal there flared to life and displayed their heading: *3112.* Bowen removed the proper disks and plugged them into the navigation computer's waiting trays. Live-feed images of their new course beamed onto the chart table's screen, and from there onto others in the Flight Deck and Monitoring Area. Those vast plumes of towering, purple gas appeared, backlit by silver stars.

The image struck Masters as resembling waves, the biggest ever created frozen in place, never to crash down.

"Navigation codes activated," said David.

"And check those radiation screens," Masters said, now at the end of his pre-launch checklist.

Anna rose from her seat in the Monitoring Area, crossed through Navigation, and approached the light propulsion engine compartment, whose core was sealed behind a dense, protective circular door.

The sign had lit and warned in flashing red letters: PHOTON DRIVE. Anna flipped a switch on the outside controls. Amber light pooled over the division between the safety door and the dual transparencies that guarded the chamber.

"Heat screens activated and operational," she called out. Then, she double-checked. The terrible certainty that she was losing her grip on reality again possessed her. Forbes, down in the subcompartment. A length of corridor wall, running where she knew open space should be. Coughing to clear her throat, Anna added, "Confirmed. Heat screens are operative."

Jane returned the copilot's checklist to its sleeve between instruments. "All checks complete."

Masters thumbed the intercom. "Standby, crew. We break orbit in—confirm time check."

"Three minutes and ten seconds," David reported.

"You heard the man. *Altares* will accelerate on a one-minute burn toward our destination. After that, we'll engage the Photon Drive. Everyone knows his or her part. Now's the time for questions if you have any."

He tipped a look toward Jane. His daughter appeared tense, as was to be expected given what they were about to attempt, but also calm and ready for the challenge. Nothing came from the others.

"All right, then. *Altares*, prepare to break orbit. Next up, a leisurely drive in the country—I think that's what they used to say."

"Two minutes, thirty seconds," David said.

Masters checked his safety harness. Behind him, Anna was back in the Monitoring Area, securing hers.

Impossible, she thought. *I didn't imagine what happened down there!*

The blue planet with its crimson-tinged impact craters, cloud cover, oceans, and mysteries, rolled beneath them.

"We'll be back," David said. "So don't go anywhere."

The boy's enthusiasm made Bowen smile. On the chart table's screen, the purple plumes held static, that distant point on the starmap promising an endless bumper of raw fuel.

"Ten seconds," David said. He counted down the rest of the way.

Altares' steering rockets kicked in, turning her prow toward the preprogrammed flight path leading along 3112.

"Pre-ignition," Masters ordered.

Jane thumbed the switch. The graceful craft rumbled around them as her colossal bell rockets fired. The light ship charged forward, breaking orbit. She arrowed in the direction of those distant plumes at a tremendous speed, her opening sprint propelling *Altares* thousands of miles in a matter of seconds. Soon, the blue planet was at their six and falling farther behind.

"How are we looking, Jane?" Masters asked.

He already knew the answer, could see the fuel gauge on their chemical propellant tanks dropping from low to the dangerous zone flagged in red.

"Maintaining burn for another twenty-five seconds," Jane said. "*Altares* on course."

"Then we must be looking good," Masters said. He matched his daughter's brave face and turned up toward the space window. All ahead looked empty, save for those distant silver stars and the swathe of purple color.

He judged their progress by how *right* the light ship felt around and beneath him — what Masters privately thought of as smooth sailing.

Altares raced on.

The chemical rockets cut out, leaving their reserves at just under five percent, according to the gauge. Enough for maneuvers, a few at least, through the steering rockets. But sub-light travel was off the table unless those gas plumes proved to be the bonanza they'd pinned their hopes upon.

The light ship carried herself ahead on momentum. The first phase of the maneuver had been accomplished. Its most critical would soon commence.

"Jane, let's rotate the particle scoop — on 448."

Jane handled the proper lever. Topside, the vane projecting out of the directional antenna took aim and began to rotate, scooping up the photons that powered their light drive.

"Four-four-eight," Jane confirmed. "Power readings are at the century mark."

Masters nodded. There was no avoiding his next action. The Photon Drive hadn't been used since before entering the black hole. His repairs to the unit, made nearly at the cost of his life, were solid, Masters told himself. But the true test would come in the next few seconds.

"Activating Photon Drive," he said.

He reached for the controls, aware of the drag imposed by their speed thanks to the power of their conventional engines. That pressure was about to magnify many times over. Masters pressed the button.

Far behind the Flight Deck, the RADIO-ACTIVE warning flashed in bold red letters on the drive chamber's door. An alarm klaxon sang out in accompaniment. The light ship's stardrive fired. Inside *Altares*, the stress increased.

"Standby," Masters called above the thunder.

Anna Bowen checked her harness. Tom Bowen drew in what would be the last easy breath until the Photon Drive disengaged. David Bowen eyed the chart table's screen—those distant plumes were the key to their return to the blue planet, which he was already pondering names for. He liked 'Treasure Island' better than any of the scientific classifications he'd thus far come up with.

The Photon Drive engaged, spewing forth a white-hot effulgence of star-born energy.

Altares shot toward her destination.

The velocity readings on the gauge above Masters' chair scrolled faster. They were cutting space at ninety-eight thousand miles-plus per second. He blinked. In that time, they'd accelerated past the hundred thousand mile mark.

The light ship's speed thrust his backbone against the pilot's chair. 129,500 now. Spelled out beneath their present velocity was what had been considered holy truth until the scoop drew in a superluminal particle—a tachyon or other exotic capable of traveling faster than light. The words read: Max Speed of 186,000 Miles Per

Second.

Up to 136,000.

The air thickened. It was all as he remembered, all as it should be. Breathing became a chore. Invisible weight pressed upon his body. The unpleasant caresses of gravity and velocity conspiring together to tear flesh from bone, teeth from jaws, deepened. Waves of pain rippled over him.

Masters tipped his head to the right, even that a struggle to accomplish. Jane was pressed against her chair. The skin of her nearest hand rippled. On his return back, he noted the wan rosy glow beyond the space window. That meant they'd reached the red end of the spectrum of the Doppler Shift. If one were able to witness *Altares'* jump across space with the naked eye, it would appear as if the light ship was crumpling in upon itself and being crushed by the fantastic stresses.

167,800.

Faster. Faster still.

Apart from the automated warning protocol in the Photon Drive chamber, none of the instruments threatened dangers, either within the ship or beyond. No asteroids lurked in *Altares'* path. No malfunctions to send them on a runaway course.

They coasted along at 178,000 miles per second, suffering the discomfort imposed by such a speed without complaint. And then, as it was designed to do, the Photon Drive cut out.

They decelerated. The *Altares* fired her steering rockets in reverse, a five-second burst that further drained her depleted reserves.

Outside windows and portholes, all of space was cloaked under a thick purple fog.

Chapter Six

They drifted through the interstellar clouds. The scoop extracted and filtered. The computer chimed its findings. Anna switched the list over to screens. Diatomatic molecules registered in alphabetical order, accompanied by their chemical symbols. Aluminum monochloride, Argonium, Carbon monoxide. The list scrolled. And there it was—H2, molecular Hydrogen!

"Track concentration," Bowen said.

Anna was already on it, and soon the trail was mapped and displayed on the chart table.

"Skipper, I hope you've got one or two course corrections up your sleeve in the Flight Deck," Bowen exclaimed.

Masters answered with a laugh. "If I have to get out and push *Altares* myself, you'll have them, Tom."

He nudged the light ship along with short bursts, and the scoop fed on thickening concentrations of hydrogen while expelling the rest of the gases and interstellar dust. The volatile gas was refined and liquefied into a more stabile form en route to the tanks. With maddening slowness, the needle ticked up and reached the edge of the red zone.

"It went a lot faster at Neptune," Jane said.

"We're a long way from Neptune. Why don't you get some rest—I'll cover the first shift."

Jane shook her head. "I'm too wired to sleep."

"Suit yourself."

"Dad, we are going back to the blue planet, aren't we?"

Masters settled back in his seat. "Of course, Jane. We're on a mission to explore. We could hardly pass up a chance to set foot on a planet that appears to be very much like our own, could we?"

Her brows furrowed. "And if it's like Earth, then what?"

There it was, the question that had dogged him for days, clearly being pondered by more than just the ship's captain.

"*Altares* is our home for now. If a better one comes along, well, we'll have that discussion then. I wouldn't pack us up just yet, though."

His answer alleviated Jane's worry,

according to her expression. Voicing it removed some of his own. It was the right answer, Masters reasoned, given that point in the discussion.

He glanced at the gauge. They were pushing closer to the edge of the red zone. On the screen, their course put them in the midst of a thick concentration of hydrogen.

"If you don't mind holding down the fort, I'd say we're due for a celebration."

He rose from the pilot's chair. When Masters returned, he carried two cups of hot tea. Jane took one. They toasted and sipped.

As with its vast library of books, *Altares'* computer was equipped with a variety of games designed for one or more players. Since leaving Delta Station, David had perused the menu, though he'd only engaged twice with the system. No, he preferred a deck of cards. The cards were real, tangible.

Of the multitude of Solitaire games, he favored Pyramid. His Nana Bowen had introduced David to the game. Only untold sums of light years and an entire universe away from her apartment outside Spaceport Alpha had he come to understand his grandmother's love of the game. It was a pursuit designed to cope with loneliness.

Nana Bowen was gone—for some long while now, according to the Time Dilation

Theory. The gloom he normally kept ahead of stung at his insides. David pulled the fresh deck of cards from the holdall and shuffled. The action and sound worked their usual soothing magic. They were reminders of home, a home so far away he'd never be able to visit it again.

He laid the cards down on his bunk in neat rows, the top consisting of a single card, and five more, all lined up to form a rudimentary pyramid shape. His objective was to remove all the cards from the pyramid to the foundation, which he built from the remaining deck.

After three hands, he sat on his bunk and shuffled the cards. David estimated that the refueling had upped past the halfway mark. By the time he returned the playing cards to his holdall and ambled back into the Navigation Area, the chart table measurement was up to seventy-eight.

"That was a quick rest," his mother said.

She sat in his seat, beside David's father. She started to rise, but he motioned for her to stay. There was something reassuring about seeing them together like that. The casual ease in which they chose to pass the time required for *Altares* to replenish her conventional fuel warmed him. Home had never been a happy realm, not that he could recall. Whether at Alpha Spaceport or after, at Beta, the invisible wall between his parents had steepened. But far from Earth, they'd found a kind of happiness he'd not seen at those other places.

"Too excited to return to the planet?" his father asked.

"You could say that."

David wandered past the chart table to the Navigation Area's porthole. The space beyond was purple soup broken by distant silver starlight. The distraction and anticipation in control of his senses was like every birthday or Christmas he'd known on Earth combined. Part of it owed to his need to exit the ship, stretch his legs, and be somewhere other than the confines of *Altares*.

The computer chirped. The chemical storage tanks were at eighty percent—a level they hadn't known since Earth's solar system.

"If you're looking for something to do," his father said, "I could use your help plotting our best course back to the blue planet."

David turned away from the view. "I'm on it."

He doubted that his father required the assistance. No, it was clear the assignment was to give David something to do. A distraction to occupy his mind. Confirming this, his parents both vacated the chart table and entered the Monitoring Area. There, their conversation resumed in whispered voices.

David set to work. Tapping buttons on the table, he mapped their return course. The screen displayed the route—*3570*. They'd traveled deep into the interstellar gas plumes to refuel on neutral hydrogen. A few corrections would put them back in orbit. And then, the long-awaited planetfall to the first extra-solar world reached by mankind could commence. David smiled.

He accessed the directional antenna and followed up his mapping with a scan. There wasn't anything in their immediate path. This star system lacked gas giants or other rocky worlds, save a few sparse asteroids in the opposite direction. But there had to be smaller debris out there, according to the impact craters that dotted the planet's landmasses. He widened the scan.

A contact flashed to their extreme north. It was still within the cloud but stationary, which meant he wasn't looking at a comet or meteor. David boosted the signal. The distant image materialized on the screen. At first he wasn't sure what he was looking at. Then the certainty struck, and a wave of cold washed over him, making it nearly impossible to speak.

David located his voice. "Captain Masters, quickly!"

Harry Masters appeared at the arch. Jane moved beside him. "What is it, David?"

David indicated the chart table screen. Masters rounded the edge and stared at the image. By then, his parents had left the Monitoring Area and were looking as well.

"What is it?" asked Jane.

"I'll try to get a better resolution," David

said.

The cameras made another zoom. More threads of purple whisked past, blocking their view.

"Scanners found it while I was plotting our return course to the planet," David said.

Bowen took his seat and thumbed switches. Long-range cameras filtered out the curtains of purple. The object swam into focus. Big. Round. Smooth.

"Is that-?" Anna gasped.

Masters nodded. "It sure looks it."

Tom Bowen leaned toward the chart table's microphone. "Let me state for the record that I am following communications protocol as set forth by the Space Authority should the *Altares* mission encounter alien intelligence."

Masters nodded and thumbed the radio. "This is Harry Masters, captain of the Earth exploration light ship *Altares*. Please respond and identify."

The alien disk brooded in silence. When no response came, Masters repeated the greeting and received the same results.

"We're still too distant to be sure, but we're not reading any power signatures aboard that alien vessel," Anna said.

"What do we do, Dad?" asked Jane.

Masters glanced around the Navigation Area, from one crewmember to the other. Then

54

he checked their refueling progress. Eight-nine percent.

"We've got another hour here," Masters said. "And then I know what I want to do. As stated, this is a ship of exploration."

He put it to a vote. The results were unanimous.

An hour and five minutes later, completely refueled, *Altares'* prow turned in the direction of the silent alien vessel.

Chapter Seven

Anna assumed radio duties as *Altares* navigated through the dense purple fog.

"This is the light ship *Altares*, origin: Planet Earth. Does anyone on the spacecraft we are approaching hear me?"

Nothing.

David tapped buttons on the computer terminal tied into the ship's directional antenna. He scanned the printout. "I think I have an answer."

"Out with it," Bowen said.

"Sensors report no active power source within that ship. She's sitting completely dead in space."

Masters realized he was holding his breath and exhaled. "We're coming in range. Anna, are you ready?"

Abandoning further attempts at

communication, Anna switched to the forward laser controls. "Targeting lock established. Laser on standby to fire."

Masters nodded. "Jane, prepare to slow us on approach. Activate steering rockets."

Jane punched in the proper buttons. "Five-second reverse burn in three...two...one."

The forward steering rockets kicked in. Those along the hull matched. *Altares* slowed her advance. Ahead, the purple gas clouds thinned, and the dark alien ship coalesced from the ether. It appeared on monitors, and as a dark smudge beyond the Flight Deck's space window.

"Power readings?" Masters asked.

"Still zero," David answered.

They neared. The image grew, solidified. The alien vessel reminded Masters of something he at first had difficulty identifying. Then his mind connected dots. Jane was younger then, five or six. They'd traveled across the Atlantic to Grand Metropolis, the mega-sprawl once known simply as Boston. Sylvia Masters was alive. It was their last vacation as a family before their time in the cottage on Rankine Lane, where his wife and Jane's mother went to paint and, sadly, die.

They'd taken a tour of the tidal habitat the Earth Authority was attempting to restore. At high tide, the ocean pounded that section of the beach, which was off limits and guarded. His Space Authority clearance got them past the security cordons. The air was briny, that small stretch of ecosystem filled with primal energy and the illusion that they'd entered an earlier world, despite the domes, towers, and bustle at their back.

They'd stayed until the tide went out, and the specialists allowed Jane to wade into one of the pools. She'd found the sand dollar shell, round in shape, with scalloped edges and circular patterns etched onto its carapace.

That was what the alien vessel reminded him of.

"Do you think it's some kind of robot ship?" Jane asked, bringing him out of the past and back to the moment.

Masters shrugged.

They assumed a slow, circular path that took them around the other spaceship. The alien giant was canted, which upon completing their first pass, revealed three perfect circular gaps in the ship's base. The distant view inside was dark and unenlightening.

"Anna, can you throw a light into that ship?"

She activated the directional antenna's spotlight and aimed its beam on the canted undercarriage. *Altares'* cameras zoomed in on what appeared to represent a kind of hangar whose walls were scored in corresponding circular lines that matched those decorating the outer hull.

"No power, no life signs," David said.

Jane faced her father. "Now what?"

They maneuvered in close. Jane gave the steering rockets another push. *Altares* came to a full stop beside the silent alien ship.

"In position," Jane said. "Autopilot engaged."

She and Masters vacated their chairs and joined the others in the Navigation Area. He could tell by the tense looks on the crew's faces what was on everyone's mind.

"Do we go over there, Skipper?" Bowen asked.

Masters eyed the porthole. Outside, set against the purple fog, the alien ship held off their starboard wing. "I think it's our duty to have a look. It's why we're out here—to learn all that we can."

"Who do you think they are—or were?" Jane said, the excitement in her voice barely contained.

Masters remembered the girl on the beach, her shrill cries and giggles at having found the sand dollar. Jane was older, yes. But she was still a girl, still excited and inquisitive about life's discoveries.

"It's possible that, whoever they were, they got caught in the black hole's pull, just like us. Maybe they ran low on fuel, too, and were trying to replenish their supply," Masters said. "Hopefully, we'll soon know more about them. Anna, as our doctor, I'd like you to join the boarding team. And David."

Jane said, "*What?*"

"I know you want to go over there, but I need you here to hold *Altares* steady."

"The autopilot can do that, Dad!"

He set his hands on Jane's shoulders and faced her not as the ship's captain, but as her father. "The autopilot won't pull the ship out of danger at an instant's notice like you can. While we're over there, I expect you and Tom to keep an eye on us. Will you promise me that?"

Frowning, Jane did. Masters turned back toward the porthole and its breathtaking view.

"All right, people. We're going over there. Let's prep Kite 1 for launch in sixty minutes. You have your orders."

The group began to disband. Bowen stayed behind at the chart table and tapped at buttons, which projected the launch coordinates for Kite 1. Jane returned to the Flight Deck. She was still a girl, but also a responsible member of his crew, Masters thought. Her mother would be proud. Then he was walking in the direction of the elevator, where the others waited.

They dressed in their atmosuits and checked horn connections with the Flight Deck.

"Any changes next door, Jane?" Masters called over the atmosuit's radio.

"None, Dad," she answered.

Even so, they would need to travel

prepared for the possibility of a dangerous encounter. Masters approached the next locker in line, which was protected by a security lock. He keyed in his code. The lock disengaged. Inside the locker were neat rows of rifles and smaller side arms, all of them powered by photons and capable of delivering an impressive punch. He removed one of the rifles and handed it to Anna, who'd finished securing the last of her atmosuit's seals.

"Boom sticks?" she asked. "Hardly a warm welcome to our new friends over there."

"I'm making the call, Anna."

She nodded and accepted the rifle. Masters pulled one of the side arms for David. He fixed the gun belt around his waist and checked the boom stick's charge before returning it to its holster. Finally, Masters selected a second rifle for his own carry before securing the locker.

They entered the Kite. Masters took to the pilot's seat. Anna wedged in beside him. David sat on the passenger's bench. The pre-flight completed, Masters thumbed the hangar release. The large bay door rolled open.

"Flight Deck, we're ready to launch."

"Kite 1, we're sending you coordinates for approach to the alien spaceship," Bowen said.

"Received."

"Good luck, Kite 1. Communications channel will remain open until you return."

"Roger that, *Altares*."

Masters released the docking clamps and magnetics, and then sent them out of the starboard hangar, into the dense purple miasma. Kite 1 dipped below the starboard wing, cleared the light ship's superstructure, and veered away, toward the alien ship.

"Scanning for any proximity changes," Anna said.

It was precautionary more than likely that their approach would trigger a reaction in the other ship. By all signs, the alien juggernaut was dead, presumably abandoned. That conclusion solidified as they neared, and the dark gaps at the base of the ship rose to view.

"There," Anna said, aiming a gloved finger toward the closest of the openings. "Those could be their version of hangar doors. Each one is uniform and identical in size."

"If they've abandoned ship, where did they go?" David asked.

"I can guess," said Masters.

He activated the Kite's searchlight. An icy white beam illuminated the alien ship's undercarriage and stabbed into the closest gap.

"You think they left for the planet?" Anna asked.

"We'll know that for sure after we make planetfall. But I'd bet it's a reasonable guess. If they navigated the black hole successfully but sustained critical damage to their systems, they might not have been left with a choice."

"Nobody's home here, that much is for

sure," David said.

Masters studied the superstructure that now dominated their view through the Kite's space window. The searchlight drifted over gray metal and grooves before again dipping up through the circular gap, into darkness. Those hangar openings were many times over the size required for the Kite to enter.

"What say you we have a look inside anyway?"

Masters gripped the controls and turned the Kite up, toward the nearest opening. Long seconds later, the alien vessel was all around them, and Masters couldn't shake the thought that it had swallowed them whole.

Chapter Eight

They passed out of the purple fog and into the cavernous underbelly. Even the Kite's spotlight couldn't fully dispel the stygian darkness inside the silent alien spaceship's lower hull. The beam thinned, forming a weak circle on the distant metal wall.

Masters turned the Kite. The beam tracked along the hull's curve, through those concentric marks etched into the gray metal.

"I don't mind saying that I feel rather small at the moment," Anna said.

"I think it's grand—the first solid proof that we're not alone in the cosmos," David added.

Masters completed the Kite's rotation. There was nothing to conflict with the belief that they'd entered the ship's hangar. The three perfect circles did, indeed, support the theory that an equal number of smaller craft had evacuated their mother ship's base. The only possible destination for those craft was the blue planet. Masters filed that notion for revisiting in the near future. The days ahead would prove or disprove the claim.

The deck appeared to run the full scope of the ship. The concentric grooves etched into the inner hull wound around, connected with other lines, and traveled up to the underbelly's ceiling.

"Anna, those depressions," Masters said.

"Some kind of power distribution network, I'd guess," she answered. "Harry, can you turn us back to eleven o'clock?"

He nudged the Kite's steering rockets. The vessel responded. The searchlight retraced its course along the gray metal wall.

"*There*," Anna said.

He saw it now, a dimple in the wall, set beneath the looping grooves. The Kite hovered. The weak, white beam stayed frozen on the depression.

"What is it, Skipper?" Bowen called over the horn.

"A way in," Masters said.

He glided them in. As the Kite neared, the dimple pulled free in the strengthening beam. It was a hatch or an airlock, oval in shape, partially opened on the darkness beyond.

"It stands to reason that they would

decompress the entire ship upon leaving," Jane said. "If they were running low on power, any atmosphere inside would eventually freeze over without artificial heat, and they wouldn't be able to return."

David said, "Clearly, they didn't."

Masters decompressed the Kite. One more check of their atmosuits, and he gave the signal. The Kite's hatch opened. They exited the ship and set foot on the canted deck.

"Power up your magnetics," Masters said.

"Already done," David answered.

Masters thumbed the switch that activated the magnetic treads in his atmosuit's boots. Walking became more of a chore, but on the march toward the airlock he was grateful to feel anchored. Without the magnetics, the sensation of moving through the dead ship was unpleasant and mildly disorienting.

"How long do you think this vessel's been out here?" David asked.

Masters' grip on the boom stick tightened. "I'd guess a long time."

The dual lights projected from each atmosuit's helmet zeroed in on the oval doorway. They approached.

"No cargo, no storage crates," Anna said. "The place looks picked clean. I'd say they executed a complete and final evacuation when they left."

"To start a new life on Treasure Island?"

Masters tipped a look at the boy. "Say

what?"

"That's the name I've given the blue planet, like in the Robert Louis Stevenson novel."

Masters cracked a smile. "X marks the spot. I like it."

The doorway into the dead ship appeared before them, taller and wider than the arches between compartments on *Altares*. Anna remarked that the ship's scale suggested a race of giants—or, certainly, forms of life bigger than humans.

Masters motioned for the others to form up behind him. The gap was easily wide enough to accommodate him walking straight through.

"*Altares*, I'm going in," he called over the horn.

Steeling himself, Masters willed his legs to move, and then he passed beyond the door.

The staircase—that's what his mind made it into—wound up from the metal floor, turned, and twisted like the impressions carved into the hangar walls. From there, the structure ascended to a raised platform high above their heads. It was the only direction leading forward.

Masters turned back to the others. "Fancy a climb?"

Anna laughed. "Good thing we wore our hiking boots."

In single file, they began to climb. Going

was slow where the staircase twisted, but the absence of gravity and their magnetic treads made the advance possible.

"Skipper, how's your progress?" Bowen asked.

"Almost there."

The lights from their helmets scattered over the staircase and glinted off the floor far below and the ceiling farther over their heads. The case widened onto the platform. As Masters stepped onto the dais, it struck him that they'd need to return down the same way when finished—and *down* was deep beneath them.

A large, oblong metal box filled the center of the dais. Its surface was carved with intricate decorative swirls.

"Are you seeing this, *Altares*?" Masters asked.

"Roger, Skipper," Bowen said. "Harry, please give the recorder a full image."

Masters moved to the base of the metal box and set his helmet's camera on full. The swirls and angles formed a kind of pattern he almost recognized—garlands of flowers, albeit alien blossoms the likes of which he'd never seen, ones with hexagonal centers and saw-tooth petals. Running down the middle, the angles formed an asymmetrical letter 'V', more harp-shaped in appearance.

"Amazing," Jane sighed over the horn.

Masters agreed. "Too bad the Space Authority is so far away. Imagine what we'd be able to learn if we towed this ship back to Delta Station for their scientists to study."

"Harry, look," Anna said.

She pointed toward a set of grooves running around the edge of the box. Masters tracked them to the base, where the lines converged.

"A release handle?" David suggested.

"Only one way to be certain."

Masters waved for the others to move back. When they were behind him, he handed his boom stick to David, leaned down, and traced the outline of the groove. An easy tug and the lever pulled away from the casing. Masters pulled harder. The release held. Another try, and he felt it give.

The decorative cover detached but remained in place.

"Anna," Masters said.

She took point at the head of the box. Masters gripped the bottom. They pulled, and the cover came free. As it lifted, revealing what the box contained, Masters' mind made the connection.

Sarcophagus, his inner voice screamed.

Anna gasped and stepped back. Masters faced the coffin's exposed insides, the lights from his helmet illuminating what the sarcophagus contained. The void had preserved the alien body. Shrouded in rich crimson fabric, its multitude of blank, rheumy eyes stared up without blinking, and seemed to curse them in silence for disturbing its long rest in the darkness.

Masters couldn't shake the sense that he'd desecrated an alien people's funerary belief system.

"I'm done my scans, Harry," Anna said.

Masters nodded. "Then let's close it up."

They drew down the lid and secured it back in place. Anna's medical kit contained samples of the dead alien's tissue, a few threads from the burial cloth, and a full body scan by the portable bio-panel in her holdall. His guilt persisted even after the sarcophagus was sealed and his inner voice reminded him that they couldn't have left the ship without following that very course of action. The entire scope of what the *Altares* mission accomplished had just doubled, *quadrupled*. Moments such as this were why they were out here.

Two hours had passed. There was more ship to explore—quite a lot, in fact. But without power to open airlocks, they'd have to search for manual releases, and the going would be slow. With air supplies down to an hour, Masters gave the order for them to return to the Kite. Besides, Masters thought on the winding path leading down to the hangar airlock, what could they possibly hope to find that could top their discovery inside the alien sarcophagus?

Kite 1 was parked where he'd left her,

and a welcome sight. They entered the ship, stowed weapons and gear, and Masters hastened through his pre-flight checklist. All systems checked out. He powered her up, guided her out of the alien flight deck, and down through the vast circular gap that had housed one of the mother vessel's three escape craft.

"*Altares*, we're on approach," Masters said into the horn.

"Welcome home, Kite 1," Jane answered.

Ahead of them, *Altares* pulled free of the purple fog. Truly, Masters thought, docking in the hangar beneath the starboard wing felt like returning home.

Chapter Nine

They were seated across from one another, Masters and the man dressed in crimson robes. A chill infused the air, the kind that steadily crept beneath his skin and into his marrow. From the periphery, he drank in the details of their surroundings. Not much, Masters saw, save for a shadowy expanse and the vast room's two occupants.

His opposite, studying him through dual sets of eyes—one smaller pair inset directly centered above the primaries—sat on a metal throne covered in elaborate decorative details. More of the hexagonal flowers with saw-tooth leaves. Masters fell into the pull of the man's eyes. Man? No. The body draped in crimson bore no resemblance to humans. The outline was more akin to terrestrial snakes, though even that wasn't accurate. The form suggested a reticulated skeleton structure, snake-like, yes, but also akin to the wings of a bat at the upper torso.

"On our planet," Masters said. The words emerged heavy and drawn out, suggesting he was dreaming. "In a place called Egypt, rulers were buried, and curses placed upon any who dared disturb their remains. Is this what we have here? You've cursed me?"

The alien visitor to his dreams shifted in place. His reticulated upper torso puffed up, more bat than asp. The surrounding darkness thrummed with a pulsing undercurrent, like a heartbeat. The cold worsened, and Masters wondered if he was back aboard the dead alien ship, on the dais, once more in the company of the corpse in the sarcophagus.

"We're explorers," Masters continued. "Opening doors—whether into entire new universes or abandoned alien vessels—is our primary mission. We meant no disrespect."

The alien monarch eyed him again. Masters noticed his opposite trembling. The icy cold was in his bones, too. So deep that the figure in crimson jerked, *clicked*, producing a sound that Masters' imagination translated into dusty, sharp bones rubbing together.

"Are you all right?" he asked.

The alien closed his eyes. Masters stood and moved closer. He reached out, intending to set his hand on the creature's approximation of a shoulder. He saw that he was wearing heavy gloves, powder blue in color, clad in his atmosuit. Instead of reticulated flesh cloaked in crimson, his fingers were on the sarcophagus lid. He pulled. The lid resisted before opening.

Don't look, he told himself.

But the dream version of Harry Masters peered down into the coffin. At first, he only saw darkness. His heart thudded—the true source of that pulsing thrum in the shadows. Then he felt its influence, dragging him closer against his will. It was the black hole, contained within the sarcophagus.

The thing hiding in the coffin came charging up, a mass of bat wings and snake bones festooned in crimson. A scream stung at his ear—Masters couldn't tell if it came from the alien or originated deep in his own throat. His vision dimmed. The scream intensified.

His eyes shot open. At first, his surroundings didn't register. The scream chased him for another fraction of a second. Masters bolted upright. He was in his bunk in the Crew's Quarters. Cold sweat soaked his brow, and his heart continued its gallop. Only a dream, he told himself. He wasn't cursed for desecrating the alien remains, but exhausted. His life had become a series of crises, one after another—malfunctioning light-speed engines, exploding red giant stars, and black holes. Their discovery of the abandoned alien spaceship in the gas plumes was monumental, but it had also contributed to his energy drain.

He swallowed down the foul taste sitting on his tongue and pressed the intercom button on the panel above his pillow. "Tom?"

Bowen answered. "You awake, Skipper?"

"Yes. Status?"

"Unchanged. Anna's working on the data you brought back from the alien ship. The chemical tanks and Photon Drive are both charged to capacity."

Masters settled the back of his head onto the sweaty pillow. "You mind running the show a little longer?"

"How much longer?"

"Enough for me to grab a shower and down a cup of hot tea?"

He heard Bowen chuckle on his way to an answer. "I think I can handle command duties until you rejoin us."

"Thanks, Tom. I owe you."

He thumbed off the intercom and stood. *Altares* hummed around him, but the melody was reassuring and the air temperature comfortable. After stretching, he approached his locker. Inside were multiple identical sets of his pale blue regulation uniform and white jacket. He picked up fresh pants, pulled a clean shirt from its hanger, and underclothes from one of two drawers. Not sure why, he opened the second. Inside that drawer was all the space on the ship allotted to personal possessions.

Beneath the framed commendation issued from the Space Authority and Masters' Silver

Star medal was a photograph of Sylvia. He'd recorded the digital image on that beach outside of Grand Metropolis on a day that now felt part of a different, lost life. His thumb brushed the screen. The 'play' button materialized under his touch and activated. The photograph renounced its fixed state, and Sylvia moved. The ocean wind swept her blonde hair. Sunglasses shielded her eyes, but he knew them to be blue behind the dark lenses. She laughed as the sudden gust tested her balance.

"Jane, be careful," Sylvia called.

Masters in the past turned the camera away and toward Jane, then five or six, clad in her colorful bathing suit, and presently engaged in the first, greatest discovery of her young life.

"Look, Mummy."

"What have you got there?" Sylvia asked, out of view.

Then-Masters aimed down at Jane. Now-Masters fought to breathe at the sight of her, all smiles, holding the sand dollar in her tiny hand. He struggled to remember her ever being so small. The Jane of today was capable of piloting the most advanced deep space probe ever launched.

"It's beautiful," Sylvia sang.

Then the eight-second video snapshot ended and reset, showing his wife on that day right before the wind kicked up. He ran his thumb along the frame and was tempted to play the sequence again. Instead, he slipped the photograph under his commendation and closed the drawer.

There were two showers in the Crew's Quarters. Like those in the subcompartment's Decontamination Area, they ran on recyclers that purified the allotment of water used, separating skin cells, hair, and other organic matter to be repurposed in the small, efficient hydroponics unit that supplied the crew with the fresh components of their diet, and the algae tanks that provided protein.

Masters stepped into the spray and dialed up the temperature. The water was mildly painful against his bare skin, but helped to wake him fully, both from his exhaustion as well as the melancholy that followed him into the shower. He lathered his skin, using the organic soap from storage. When he was done, he turned on the jets. Warm air blown from vents dried his body. Eyes closed, he imagined himself back on the beach, Sylvia laughing as the wind attempted to knock her off her feet, Jane in the tidal pool.

"I miss you, Syl," he whispered.

Saying the words removed the unwanted weight that had piled onto his shoulders since the return from the abandoned alien spaceship. He dressed in his fresh uniform, sent the former into the laundry chute for cleaning, and emerged again composed.

The view out the Monitoring Area porthole showed only purple fog. Anna Bowen was bent over the bioscope. She righted when he entered.

"Anything interesting to report?" he asked.

She smiled and switched the scope's view onto the wall screen. "In fact, yes."

The image showed red streaks.

"Fibers from the alien's burial shroud," she said. "They're plant-based, according to properties that very much match our own Earth flora."

"And our late friend over there?" He tipped his chin in the imagined direction of the dead alien ship.

She punched buttons. The view on the monitor altered, becoming a computer diagram of the alien. The representation stood beside a human for contrast—a full meter above the man's head. Cutaways showed what Masters assumed were internal organs, as well as the reticulated skeleton system, which tapered down to fan-shaped lower limbs.

"There are internal details we recognize, like air sacs, a circulatory system, bones. Lots of bones," she said. "And others I can't even begin to guess the nature of. As to who he or his people are…"

Her voice trailed off, the question left

unanswered.

"Maybe his friends can tell us, on the planet," Masters said.

He clapped a hand on Anna's shoulder on his way through the arch and into the Navigation Area. That side of *Altares* still faced the alien colossus. The dead ship was visible through the porthole.

"Are we going over there again, Skipper?" Bowen asked. He glanced at the porthole, indicating the dead ship.

Masters was sure there was more to be learned on the abandoned spacecraft. But then he remembered the dream. It was a ship of ghosts, a memorial. For all he knew, it was also their version of sacred ground. Besides, there was more to be learned about them and their plight by pressing forward.

"No, Tom, not for now," he said.

Masters turned toward the Flight Deck. The version of Jane seated at the copilot's controls was more than twice the age of the girl splashing around in the tidal pool on Earth captured in that eight-second snapshot.

"Jane, prepare to take us out," he said. "We're making our way back to the planet."

Chapter Ten

Altares charged out of the swirling purple bands, a blur of red at the lead of a pristine white comet's tail. The light ship arrowed across the gulf of empty space, her prow aimed in the direction of the blue planet.

174,000 miles per second, according to the velocity gauge, Masters saw when he lifted his eyes. The severe discomfort was back, with gravitational forces determined to rip flesh off bones and flatten his spine against the back of his pilot's chair. Pain flared in his jaw. That, Masters realized, owed to him grinding his teeth. He willed his jaw to relax and gripped the chair's arms. The ripples caressed his knuckles, stabbed at his cheeks. The alien ship was at their six now. It was a brilliant discovery, unprecedented. So why was he so unnerved by opening that sarcophagus?

He shook his head. The powerful force dug against his face.

"Dad?" Jane asked from his right. "Are you okay?"

He nudged his eyes back toward her. As he expected, Jane was rigid in the copilot's chair, her safety harness secured. The invisible hands scrambling over his flesh were attacking hers, dimpling Jane's forehead and part of her throat.

Masters said he was and reached over, clamping his right hand over her left. They held on that way for long seconds, neither speaking as the warning trilled from the Photon Drive chamber and the air pulsed with primal energy.

The drive deactivated, as it was instructed to, and *Altares* slowed. The light ship continued forward on momentum. The agony cut out with the Photon Drive, and breathing became easy once more.

Masters faced the space window. Beyond the reinforced panel, the blue planet was just visible in the distance, an azure point set against the black velvet starmap.

"We're on approach," Bowen called from the Navigation Area. "We'll be in range to assume a high orbit in three hours."

The far-away blue dot steadily grew, and with it so did Masters' enthusiasm. This had been a mission of firsts from its beginning. Soon, the crew of *Altares* would earn another: visiting an Earth-like world an entire universe beyond their mother planet's solar system.

Jane checked gauges. Masters confirmed their speed and trajectory. *Altares* sailed toward her destination.

Anna readied the injections.

"Pana-vac," she said when she caught David's worried look. "Immunity booster. It's just a precaution."

He entered the Monitoring Area, whose screens once more projected the blue planet via the live feed coming in through the chart table. "But I thought we weren't exposing ourselves to the planet's air, that we'd be in full atmosuits for the duration of our time on the surface?"

"That's right," Anna said. "Which is as much for your Treasure Island's benefit as it is for ours."

David smiled at the nod to his nickname for the planet. "So we don't contaminate the environment down there."

Anna picked up the first of the five syringes. "We don't want to leave our bacteria or viruses behind anymore than we want to bring theirs back with us. Ready?"

David drew in an audible breath. "Yes, more than ready."

He removed his jacket. She injected his upper arm. David didn't flinch, yet one more reason to admire her son.

"How is the global mapping coming?"

David lowered his sleeve and pulled on

his jacket. "We begin mapping on the next orbit. We'll chase the daylight and should have a detailed surface scan within the next thirty hours."

"Wonderful."

"And from there, we can determine the best places to investigate and land. Exciting, isn't it?"

"Very," Anna said. "But after exploring an abandoned alien spaceship, that planet will need to provide some fairly interesting sights if it hopes to come close."

She smiled and picked up the tray upon which the remaining doses rested.

In the Navigation Area, Masters leaned over the chart table, the look on his face easy to translate.

"You're sure, Tom?" he asked.

Bowen ran through the spectrum a third time. "Sure, Skipper. We're not picking up any response to our welcome broadcast, not on any frequency. There's just dead air down there."

"Unless those three support craft were capable of interstellar travel," Anna said. She motioned for Masters to remove his jacket. He tensed as the needle's tip punctured skin. "Baby."

Masters scowled. "No, I'd bet those smaller ships are like our Kites—designed to support the mother vessel and only for short-range use."

"Then they must be down there," Bowen

said. "Along with our mysterious alien friends."

His turn, Bowen removed his jacket and suffered the sting in silence.

"Put the welcome broadcast on automatic," Masters said. "Let's give them some time to pick it up and respond before we show up on their doorstep for tea."

Bowen flashed a smile and followed through on the order. The greeting looped.

"We'll be starting to map, Skipper. But I'll keep an eye out for welcome mats."

"You do that," Masters said. "David, Jane, could you come in here, please?"

The two youngest members of the crew joined them around the chart table, whose screen displayed the blue planet.

"Regarding the first team to head down to Treasure Island," Masters said. "I'm sure that if I asked for volunteers, five hands would get raised."

Jane excitedly raised hers. David followed, a close second.

"Protocol suggests there always be a minimum of two crew members aboard—one pilot and a mission specialist in support," he continued. "Remember, this is just a first look. There will be excursions down there for anyone not included on the initial planetfall team."

Jane's excitement deflated. She lowered her hand.

"Jane, since I went over to the alien spacecraft, I volunteer to man the Flight Deck,"

Masters said.

"Really?"

He nodded. Jane hugged him.

"As for the rest of our planetary team—it needs the eye of a skilled explorer."

Masters faced David. The boy looked ready to hoot. Instead, David lowered his hand and nodded, "Aye, Captain."

"Finally, Tom. I'd trust this mission to you."

Their eyes connected, and Bowen knew what Masters really meant—that he trusted Jane's safety to him. Bowen stood and extended his hand. The two men shook.

"So, Anna, if you don't mind holding down the fort with me..."

She set a hand on David's shoulder. "It'll be difficult, but I think I can wait for the next visit."

"Okay, people, we're on the clock. Tom, how about you get working on that surface map so you know where you'll be landing."

"Straight away, Skipper," Bowen said.

Altares circled the planet, her eyes trained and narrowed on the ground below. The surface map generated on the chart table in increments, one oblong patch of detail at a time, like an old-style quilt being stitched together from pieces. The majority of the land mass appeared to be comprised of rocky desert terrain, dustbowl, and regolith. Along those cratered chains, Bowen detected the first notation of curiosity.

"There, around the crater walls, that distinct crimson color," he said. "Does it look familiar?"

Masters shook his head. "No."

"We're looking at the lungs of the planet. Why there's a perfect balance of oxygen and carbon dioxide. That combination is from plant life. And not just any flora."

He zoomed in the camera view. The image was startling in its clarity. Presented on the screen was a field of fat crimson flowers with hexagonal centers and saw-tooth petals.

Masters folded his arms. "Now that you mention it, I do recognize them."

"You should," Bowen said. He flipped a switch and a smaller window opened beside the survey map image. The pull-down showed helmet camera footage of the alien sarcophagus. "I'd bet my seat on the Kite that they're one and the same, and that they match the plant fiber used for the dead alien's funeral robe."

"That means they're down there."

"Or they were," Bowen said. "And judging by the scope of how much habitat those flora now occupy, I'd say for a very long time."

Less than an hour later, the survey map picked up its second detail worth noting.

"Skipper, Jane, Anna, I suggest you all return to the Navigation Area," Bowen called over the intercom.

Anna hastened in from the Monitoring Area, where she was inventorying the medical field kit for the planetfall mission, Masters and Jane from the Flight Deck.

"We've just picked it up on the cameras," David said.

Bowen transferred the image to the main wall screen. Masters turned. Even before Jane spoke the words, he knew it for what it was.

His daughter said, "It's a city!"

Chapter Eleven

A city. A very old city, one older than the ancient centers at Cairo, Athens, and Rome on Earth, around which the modern mega-metropolises sprawled. Even from orbit, Bowen guessed it had been there for centuries—likely millennia. As the Kite raced down through the clouds and he got his first close-up look at their destination, his theory was confirmed.

The structure rose up from a basin of fractured and time-smoothed rock, near what appeared to be a dry riverbed. That figurative stone road wound through a section of the ancient structure, leading him to believe the location had been intentional, and that the river had dried up well before their arrival or was seasonal, slated to return during seasons of heavy rain.

The city was impressive, even in its

decay, with eroded spires stretching as high into the sky as anything that had existed on Earth before their departure.

"Incredible," Bowen said into the horn. "It has to be as big as Space Station Delta."

"Or Epsilon Station, to be exact," Anna countered.

Space Station Epsilon had only been a shell, far from completion, before *Altares'* launch. But Epsilon was designed as the biggest structure in Earth orbit, and he bought the analogy.

Epsilon's planetary comparison was laid out in an asymmetrical grid pattern, with the tallest structures at the center, fanning out and shortening in height to the city limits. Several of the buildings had toppled, taking others down with them. The metal had a dull, oxidized appearance that matched the surrounding scree. More than likely, the materials had been harvested and refined from the land the city sat upon. No power signals registered from the structures. It was, Bowen sensed, a city of the dead.

"Do you think our alien friends built that?" David asked from the Kite's passenger bench.

Bowen pondered the question as Jane circled the city's perimeter from 800 meters above the basin. "I don't know for certain, but at first glance I'd say no, David."

David left his seat and crowded between

the pilot and copilot. "Explain, Dad."

"For a start, the alien ship we encountered in the plumes. What common geometric shape determined so much of their technology?"

"The circle," David said.

"Exactly. It was a recurring factor—the shapes of the doorways, the three hangar openings in the lower deck, even the design of their vessel. The city below us shows none of that mindset."

David gazed out the Kite's space window. They were cutting alongside one of the fallen spires. Through the gap, he glimpsed the distant shore of the planet's major ocean. Closer in that same direction, a field of crimson alien flowers shattered the endless beige terrain.

"Is it possible that there were *two* alien civilizations on this planet?" David asked.

Jane glided the Kite farther out. They were over the dry riverbed now.

"We now know that we aren't the only travelers who were forced through the black hole. On this side of the vortex, the exit point deposits anything drawn in within range of your Treasure Island, so it's reasonable to think others have come here before us."

"So where have they gone?" asked Jane.

For this question, Bowen didn't have an answer.

He drew in a deep breath. The atmosuit suddenly felt constrictive and burdensome.

"Jane, make another pass. Then let's see about landing and having a look in person."

Jane nodded and banked the Kite.

Planetary data poured in from both the ground team and *Altares'* scanners in orbit. A familiar image formed on the screen in the Monitoring Area—the planet, dissected by the light ship's thermal lenses. Anna tapped buttons. Crust, mantle, and molten core were identified, along with northern and southern magnetic poles that radiated waves outward to surround the planet in a protective shield against its sun's deadly emissions.

She made several notes on her tablet. Treasure Island was a textbook habitable planet according to human standards. So why was it so silent, so empty apart from one confirmed species of plant life? And that one flora, by their research, wasn't native to the blue planet. It was invasive, a transplant from other, earlier visitors.

It's like a blank template, she thought. A world waiting to be claimed and shaped in the claimer's image.

Footsteps approached. Anna set down her tablet and looked up to see Masters standing at the arch. That meant *Altares* was flying on autopilot.

"Sort of quiet up here now," he said.

Anna agreed. Since the planetfall team's departure, a lonely sensation had fallen over

Altares. The background chatter of the instruments grew more pronounced. The ship felt larger, emptier. A similar malaise, according to his expression, affected Masters.

"The information coming in is extraordinary," she said. "Take a look."

Masters shuffled into the Monitoring Area and scanned the cutaway image. "Extraordinary, yes. And even more of a mystery."

"Only one?" she said, intending the comment to sound light.

Masters' frown deepened. "Why is that city empty? If our friends from the alien spaceship didn't build it, then who did? And where did they go? We know they were here. Like Tom said, the lungs of the planet—a natural system of manufacturing oxygen and removing carbon dioxide exists down there as a direct result of their seeding the desert."

"Maybe that empty city has the answers." She glanced at the screen's clock. "They'll be setting down for a look in a few minutes."

"Yeah," Masters said.

Anna started toward the Navigation Area. At the arch, Masters spoke her name. Anna halted and turned back.

"It's just us up here for the moment. Is something wrong?"

"Wrong?" she parroted.

"Since we came upon this planet—the repairs—you've seemed out of sorts."

There was so much to say in response to his prodding: that she didn't trust her memories, which no longer matched up against today's facts; that she questioned her own sanity, not merely over missing rooms but the appearance of a ghost spouting offers of a second chance. She tensed. Her quivering lower lip betrayed the rest of her façade.

"Anna, tell me."

"Jim Forbes, here on *Altares*?"

His question made her regret answering. Embarrassment rose red up Anna's throat and stained her cheeks. "You don't believe me?"

"I—"

She turned away and continued to the chart table, where she took her husband's seat. "I don't fault you for that, Harry. I don't believe myself. But I tell you, insane as it sounds, there was a storage space in that section of the ship after we made the Neptune maneuver, and whether or not it was a ghost, I saw Jim Forbes down there in Subcompartment D."

Masters neared David's seat but didn't take it. She sensed his eyes on her, though not in judgment.

"I believe you," he said.

Anna looked up. "You do?"

Masters nodded and flashed a reassuring smile. "Why wouldn't I? You're the smartest, finest doctor, and the only one I'd have picked for my crew. None of us would have made it this far if not for you."

A wave of relief washed over her. She'd carried the burden of the secret for days. The weight lifted.

"Skipper," Bowen cut in over the horn.

Masters finally sat in David's chair. "Receiving you, Tom."

"We're on the ground. And a fine landing it was."

The screen altered, showing the live camera feed from Kite 1. The view through the copilot's window stabilized on a patch of arid soil, above which the alien city's outlying buildings rose.

"A momentous occasion, *Altares*," Bowen continued. "Men have walked on the mother planet's moon, on Mars, numerous of Jupiter's satellites, and various of the asteroid belt's planetoids, like Ceres. But we are the first of our race to set foot on a world outside of our own solar system."

An icy-hot emotion flickered through Masters' insides. "How about you mark this moment in time, Tom, with a grand statement."

"You mean something along the lines of, 'One giant leap for mankind'?"

"Unless you've got something better in mind."

He heard Bowen exhale. "That's already been done. No, I think in this case we'll take a different route, Skipper. A dedication, perhaps, from each of us. Jane, you go first."

Bowen tipped a look toward his pilot. Jane, in her atmosuit with the blue details, appeared on the screen.

"I dedicate this first manned landing on a planet outside Earth's solar system to Sylvia Masters—wife, friend, painter, and mother."

The emotion intensified. "Good work, Jane," Masters said.

"And you, David?" Bowen invited.

David replaced Jane as the subject of Bowen's helmet camera. "I dedicate the steps I am about to take to Jim Hawkins, my predecessor on adventures to distant, strange lands."

"That only leaves me," said Bowen.

He exited the copilot's seat. The camera tracked him to the Kite's hatch. Beyond the airlock, the alien planet and its silent city awaited.

"I dedicate this first manned landing on extra-solar firmament to the most beautiful and wonderful woman it's been my honor to know—my wife, Anna Bowen."

On the screen, Bowen reached his gloved hand toward the keypad. He thumbed one button, and then a second. The airlock released. Bowen stepped out of the Kite and into the alien planet's resplendent daylight.

Chapter Twelve

Bowen switched the atmosuit's horn over to external as well as its continuous link up to the *Altares*. The low sough of the planet's breeze drifted in. At first, he imagined it as a sound from the countryside, one that would be rich with the lush, green fragrance of woods and meadow. Soon, its emptiness reminded him of a ghost's baleful moan, a reminder that they now walked a haunted and potentially dangerous realm.

The terrain underfoot was solid, a mix of cracked shale that the wind had filled in with dust and sand. The sun beating down warmed his face and heated his skin. The atmosuit compensated, keeping the temperature inside comfortable. A strange and beautiful place surrounded him.

"Power readings still negative," David

said.

Bowen glanced over to see his son had a tablet aimed at the way directly ahead—the city's limit. Here, most of the outlying spires remained upright. He guessed these to be in the five- to ten-story height range. Others deeper in soared up to ten times that stature, and many of the tallest had come down, creating spectacular wreckage.

Bowen's grip on the boom stick tightened. "David, I appreciate your devotion to fact gathering, but please stay focused on your surroundings."

David swept the tablet across the horizon, widening his scan. "Yes, Dad."

"I meant..." Bowen caught himself smiling. "Never mind, carry on with your investigation."

His son was outfitted with a side arm, still holstered. Jane Masters had her boom rifle raised and ready. Not that there was anything living or technological to fear here, according to their data. No birds, reptiles, or living creatures apart from the saw-tooth flowers claimed the planet as their home. Given the lack of pollinating insects, he guessed the flowers reproduced by putting forth chutes or runners, self-replicating like some earth plant species. Of course, pollination and other known analogies didn't necessarily apply on Treasure Island. This was a planet far from Mother Earth.

He ambled forward and tipped another

look at David. To his son, the planet had more than lived up to its namesake in terms of riches. Had they remained on Earth or returned following their successful mission to Alpha Centauri, David likely would have risen high through the ranks of the Space Authority. Bowen saw his son, as a man, in command of Space Station Delta or the new Epsilon Station. Here, David Bowen was in charge of so much more.

"Tom?" Masters said, pulling him out of his thoughts.

"Here, Skipper."

"Can you turn your helmet camera left—to seven o'clock?"

Bowen did. Among the time-eroded metal surfaces was what appeared to be a door leading in, invisible from the distance and angle of their approach, but now clear for what it was.

"*Eureka*," Bowen said.

He adjusted his course.

While the planetary information continued to stream in and was fed into *Altares*' computer, Masters called up the ship's schematics. The light ship was a wonder of design and engineering, and even her blueprints impressed him. With Anna working in the Monitoring Area and the ground team moving closer to accessing the city's insides, he drifted over the imagery projected onto a second window on the chart table's screen.

Detachable forward command module/life raft. Water storage tanks. Docking access hatch.

He followed the ship's design past the starboard hangar containing one of the light ship's two support craft, into Subcompartment D, scene of Anna's ghostly encounter. Masters knew *Altares* better than anyone, even her designers. He'd taken her on both inter-solar system test cruises, and had flown her farther than those who'd dreamed her up dared dream possible. But the person who knew *Altares* better than anyone with the exception of Harry Masters was Anna Bowen. The facts didn't add together. He remembered her mentioning the Neptune maneuver — their first refueling mission to replenish *Altares'* chemical fuel supplies. The eighth planet from the sun boasted eighty-percent hydrogen in the vibrant blue soup of its thick outer atmosphere. The planet also put up the fastest and most violent wind speeds ever recorded in the solar system — 1,300 mph.

If Anna said there was cargo storage room in that part of the ship…

"*Altares*, you still there?" Bowen asked.

Masters faced the other image on the screen. Bowen's helmet camera was aimed high at the nearest tower set against an expanse of cloudless blue sky.

"Right here, Tom."

The picture tracked down to the vacant

doorway, now maybe twenty meters ahead. The shape of the entrance formed a rough trapezoid, set upright. The panel had fallen out of its frame, creating a crude welcome mat among the other piles of decaying metal scattered about the bare rock courtyard.

"I'm mostly certain that the place won't come crashing down on our heads within the next hour," Bowen said. "Since that's when our oxygen tanks will need to be replenished, the plan is to be back at the Kite no later than fifty-nine minutes from now. *Mark*."

Masters smiled, his search for missing storage rooms now on hold out of necessity. "Be careful."

"Always," Bowen said. Then he advanced toward the entrance.

Bowen passed under the city's shadow. The alien sun's warmth and glare cut out. The wind's sough lost its pleasant illusion and again transformed into the disembodied, malevolent howl that haunted old houses back on Earth. Something about the surrounding structure activated comparisons.

Factory, Bowen thought.

The same wind that had forced the door had scattered sand into the entrance. He crunched over the grains. Ahead, the metal floor matched the exterior, oxidized by time and the elements. This section of the city's innards was open, angular. Above him, a roof with indentations soared some two full stories over their helmets.

"You heard Captain Masters. Be careful," Bowen said. "Walk with caution."

Leading the way, he crossed the sand-strewn floor. Beyond the entrance, light spilled down from gaps in the ceiling. The way ahead widened. Now, the ceiling looked to be five or more stories above them, cathedral-like in its scope and design, with much taller steeples aimed skyward. Running straight down through the floor in several locations were enormous cylinder-shaped constructs.

Yes, a factory, Bowen thought. *But manufacturing what?*

David moved beside him, the tablet once more aimed around at their surroundings. "Analysis confirms it—the metal here does not match that of the alien vessel. We're looking at an entirely different technology."

"David, scan those tubes," Bowen said. He tipped his helmet in the direction of the nearest cluster of cylinder shapes.

David did as instructed. "According to sensors, those structures extend deep underground."

"How deep?"

David checked the readings. "Deeper than the hand unit can track, Dad."

Masters chimed in over the horn. "Is it possible that they're some kind of geothermal conduit designed to draw energy from the planet's core?"

"That's a good call, Harry," Bowen said. "The place is riddled with them. If the entire city is laid out like this section of the grid, it must have been extracting an enormous amount of power from underground heat."

"To do what?" Anna asked.

"There's the question," said Bowen.

David lowered the tablet. "Do we keep going farther?"

"A little ways, yes," Bowen said.

Raising his boom rifle, he marched forward. The next section mirrored those already crossed, but the scope was vaster, nearly overwhelming in its largeness. Clusters of the cylindrical constructs soared up ten stories over their heads. One entire section of distant roof had collapsed, permitting sunlight to rain down from the rectangular patch of exposed blue sky. The metal floor continued, but was broken into pathways leading over drops into darkness.

They could have flown *Altares* through here, Bowen mused, even as slight vertigo tickled his belly.

From the cut of his eye, he saw Jane direct toward the edge of the platform, which was guarded by a length of time-eroded safety rail.

"Jane, no—get away from there," Bowen ordered.

Jane obeyed, and started back toward him.

Before the crack sounded through the horn, Bowen felt the platform quiver under his treads, the stress of frail metal giving way telegraphed through magnetics, reinforced fibers, skin, and bone.

Lowering his rifle, Bowen made a grab for Jane. A second later, the platform collapsed, and they were falling into shadows.

Chapter Thirteen

For a terrible instant, there was nothing but darkness running deep below, and the certainty of a drop to their deaths in an unfathomably distant alien version of Hell. But Bowen's instincts kicked in, and he powered up the atmosuit's boots to full power. The magnetics activated, and he found enough iron in the floor to latch hold on. Gravity slammed into Bowen, and exquisite pain erupted from his ankles and shins. But instead of spilling down into the abyss, he was still connected to the ground level platform. Even more important, he'd caught Jane around the waist.

"*Tom*," Masters shouted. "Tom, respond!"

Bowen sucked in a deep breath and tipped his head down, so that the helmet's camera no longer sent a vision of shadows up to *Altares*, but that of his prize.

"Jane, thank God," Masters said over the

horn.

"We shouldn't be thanking the Almighty just yet," Bowen said.

One of the platform's supports had let go. In facing Jane, he gleaned an intricate series of metal gantries and catwalks running down deep into the lower levels. The one his soles clung to had bent under their weight but was likely to snap after more stress was placed upon it. He hauled Jane back.

"Magnetize your boots," Bowen ordered.

Jane nodded. As soon as she was parallel to him, she followed through. Some of the pressure on Bowen's bones vanished, though not all. Gravity reminded him that he needed to move.

"Now what?" Jane asked.

If they were in space or some other microgravity setting, the answer would be easy: reduce magnetics on one boot, shuffle back, reengage, repeat with other boot all the way back to solid footing. It would be slow going, but certain to work. Here, the same wasn't feasible because of gravity's push and pull.

"Tom, what's happening?" Anna cut in.

What was happening was that he was staring at the dark interior of the planet, and very much wishing to be out of there.

"David," Anna called before he could answer. "Where's David?"

In his haste to grab hold of Jane before she fell, he'd forgotten about his son. Fresh panic engulfed Bowen.

"David," he called.

David didn't answer.

Had the boy gone over the edge of the abyss? Cold sweat broke across Bowen's forehead. He screamed David's name.

"Tom, bio-panel readings show him back on the surface, just departing the Kite," Anna said.

He's alive, Bowen thought. Relief washed over him.

"Dad," David called "Grab hold, I'll help you up!"

A length of heavy-tensile rope appeared between Bowen and Jane.

Bowen slowly inhaled. "Good work, David. Now Jane, you go up first. When you're on the platform, help David and I'll follow."

Jane nodded, shouldered her boom rifle by its strap, and gripped the rope. Going backwards for the first few steps, Jane pivoted around and ascended the remainder of the distance at a brisk clip. By then, the seconds had drawn out, grown long. Every shake of the aged metal beneath his treads signaled its looming collapse in Bowen's imagination. And during those seconds, his helmet's camera recorded.

"Okay, Dad," David said.

Tom reached for the rope. He released, turned, and reactivated magnetics. Both Jane and David steadied the line, which David had anchored somewhere beyond his field of vision—the opposite safety rail, he guessed. Bowen ascended higher, aware of the shaking underfoot, and also of his racing pulse.

"You're almost there," Jane said.

"Just a little more, Dad."

Bowen pulled himself up, sure that if the metal under him didn't snap first, his bones would. He reached the ramp's fold that had spared their lives, crossed over it, and stood again on the platform, back in the light.

"Hurry," Bowen said. "We're getting out of here."

David unfastened the rope and wound it up. Then, together, the three members of the ground team hurried out of the city and back to the Kite.

They recharged their suits' atmosphere tanks. The silent city towered above them, and Bowen fought his fear that it was ready to collapse and bury them alive at any second.

"You can see that there are dual functions in those structures," David said, pointing at the image of the vast interior on the screen. "Intake and exhaust ports. One functions to inhale, the other to exhale."

Masters listened, still tense from the near-disaster inside the ancient city. "Like lungs. *Lungs of the planet*," he said. "I'm quoting you, Tom, on the flora left behind by our alien friends. But the aliens who built that city were

107

here first. What if it's some kind of terraforming complex?"

Bowen pondered the other man's words. "Built by the first race to visit this world. Those tubes extend deep into the planet's crust. It could be that their design was to extract subsurface water or ice to make the atmosphere breathable, while the intakes filtered out toxic gases."

"Which would mean that twice, now, different alien races have attempted to terraform this planet and colonize it," Jane said. "And both times they failed."

Silence briefly settled between the ground team and *Altares*.

"Jane, you sure that you're all right?" Masters asked.

"I'm fine, Dad, thanks to Mister Bowen."

Masters leaned forward and closed his eyes. "Thanks, Tom."

Bowen nodded, but said nothing. Words, in this case, weren't necessary.

Anna entered from the Monitoring Area. Masters opened his eyes and righted.

"There's something down there."

The plan wasn't to go back inside. After recharging their atmosuits, Bowen would take them to their second objective: the nearest of the chain of impact craters overflowing with crimson flora, and from there they'd hop on over to the seashore and take water samples. With the first stage of planetfall accomplished, they'd then head back to the light ship. Any subsequent ground team missions would be Masters' call, and likely comprised of the Skipper and Anna.

Anna sent the feed through to the Kite's screen. He knew the moment too well—one second, he was upright, the next clutching onto Jane, his boots magnetized, his skeleton in agony as gravity shoved down on his weight. The helmet camera was aimed into the abyss beneath the city.

"*There*," Anna said, and froze the image.

The picture was grainy, distorted. It showed the darkness barely lit by the beams from the atmosuit's helmet and what little glow made it through the punctured ceiling. Below them, the maze of gangways laddered up and down. He thought about David's reference to the planet—Treasure Island. The alien world was much more like something out of Verne than Stevenson. He was looking down at the center of the Earth.

Anna focused in on the anomalous object sprawled across one of the catwalks. Even out of focus, he made the connection.

"Look familiar?" she asked.

Based on David's scans, he was certain they could access the lower level by more direct and less dangerous means.

"The intake cylinders," he said. "Look at those grooves, like rungs. I'm confident we could descend down to the next level safely that way."

"Safely?" Bowen said. He laughed, though not in dismissal of his son's suggestion. The danger posed by the vast alien structure, city or terraforming center regardless, made the term meaningless.

"We have to check it out," Anna said. "Even if it's you and I, Harry."

"No," Bowen said. "David's right, and we're already here on the ground. We certainly can't go on without knowing more about what happened here."

"Just be careful, Tom," Masters said. "All of you."

"Roger that, Skipper."

Masters and Anna exchanged a look. The mysterious image hovered on the chart table screen, static and demanding their focus.

"Let's move out, Team," Bowen said.

Soon, the three figures were back on alien soil and marching toward the entrance point.

The image on the chart table's screen dimmed and then wavered before surging back.

"What was that?" Masters asked.

"I'm not sure. A power fluctuation."

"Source?"

Anna moved to the wall of computers and tapped at buttons. She scanned the computer printout, all emotion ironed off her

face.
"What is it, Anna?" Masters asked.
"A one-second energy drain."
"From where?"
"Subcompartment D."

Chapter Fourteen

Hand rungs. Which meant the first inhabitants had hands, or an approximation.

"Unlike the Rets," said David.

"Rets?" Bowen parroted.

"Reticulated. It's easier than referring to them as 'second inhabitants' or 'the aliens from the ship'."

"Your Treasure Island's certainly turning into quite the melting pot of space people," Bowen said.

They reached the giant cylinder, whose rungs for hands or approximations led down into the abyss. The sunlight streaming through the vast gap in the distant ceiling was at a different angle now. The fresh break in the floor allowed more of it to spill deeper, which partially illuminated the lower recesses. It was likely, Bowen thought, that the elements pouring in through the gap over the course of untold centuries had weakened the platform's metal enough for their weight to bend it.

"Onward," he said, and led the way.

The rungs were solid, molded into the metal and out of direct contact with the elements feasting on that exposed patch of the dead city. The spaces were farther apart—not a problem for a man of Bowen's height, but for the others, especially David, the gap between holds would require them to stretch.

With the boom rifle strapped around his shoulder, Bowen descended. He tried to not think of the action as heading lower into another planet's version of Hell. A glance out the face shield of his helmet challenged his resolve. Light poured down, but it was soon gobbled up and rendered useless by angles and lines and the multitude of layers that crisscrossed the city's underbelly. *City.* According to theory, their city was in all likelihood a terraforming station, its metals sourced from the surrounding scrabble, its elements mined from beneath the planet's surface. According to the planetscape outside its crumbling exterior, its builders had succeeded in their task. Treasure Island might once have been as inhospitable as Venus or Pluto, but now it was a mirror image of the Earth apart from its lack of biodiversity and intelligent life forms.

Twice, different species had tried to stake their claim here. And twice, also according to data, they'd failed.

What Anna saw on the helmet's camera

was likely to provide more answers as to why. First, his focus belonged to his two crewmates.

Bowen reached the platform and tested it with his right foot. The metal seemed sturdy. He stepped onto it and stomped his boots.

"Dad?" David spoke over the horn.

"It's stable. Come on down, but be careful of the rungs. They're solid, but farther apart than ideal for human hands."

David made it down without difficulty, stretching out between handholds. Jane was more graceful. The three turned in the direction of the oddity glimpsed on Bowen's helmet camera.

They moved slowly, cautiously, along the gangway. The metal groaned at times, but held.

"Be ready to magnetize your boots—don't wait for my order," he said.

"And *that?*"

Jane extended the muzzle of her boom rifle in the direction of their destination. Bowen tracked it past shadow, into the broken sunlight spilling down on that section of the under-city.

"Approach with caution."

He led the way toward it. The oddity, laid out across that section of catwalk, glittered in the sunlight, likely for the first time in millennia. As they neared, Bowen's instincts proved correct. The alien corpse had looked like a skeleton in the helmet camera's quick scan, but up close, in the sunlight reaching deep into the abyss, he knew they weren't gazing upon remains made of bone. These were metallic in composition.

"It's just like the Ret's skeleton structure," said Jane.

"No, not exactly. There are significant differences," David corrected.

His son had the tablet out and was scanning the remains. Yes, Bowen agreed, the object looked like the alien skeletal structure that Anna had projected onto the screen following her analysis, but the imagery presented here was more than ribs and bones picked clean by time. The metal version also maintained its joints and tendons, which kept the skeleton whole. Its head was intact, its dual sets of eyes cinched shut. There were other differences, like hooked projections out of the chest ribs where the Rets took on their bat's wing comparison.

"Those almost look like weaponry," Bowen said.

A chill teased the nape of his neck. He fought it, failed. The shiver skipped down his backbone.

"David," Anna chimed in, "can you get a metallurgical analysis?"

"Prepare to receive, *Altares*."

Even before David ran the study, Bowen questioned the oddity's composition. It looked mostly Ret—including the gray color of the metal they'd scanned in the abandoned spaceship. But around its edges, the skeleton had oxidized, lending it the same look of distress as the dead city.

Curious," David said. And then he confirmed Bowen's observation. "It's Ret technology and alloy, but it's also got properties of the first colonists' tech."

"A hybrid?" Jane asked.

Bowen pondered the question. "I suppose its conceivable that the Rets landed, found this complex like we did—only a great deal sooner in its timeline, perhaps still in a viable state—and then took control of it."

"To finish its purpose," said Anna. "To complete the terraformation of Treasure Island."

"Yes," Bowen sighed. "Mission accomplished."

"Switching to thermal scan," David said.

He tapped at buttons with his gloved pointer and then aimed the tablet at the metal skeleton. Bowen watched from over the boy's shoulder. The screen was a wash of warm colors—sunny yellows edged in red, representing the flood of light and warmth raining down through the newest gap in the ceiling. The metal skeleton registered as green. Among the articulated bat wings, those metal protuberances glowed a pale blue.

"David," Bowen gasped.

"I see it—registering a power source within that device, probably fed by solar energy."

"Back to the Kite, at once," Bowen said.

Jane guarded David as he moved away, her boom rifle aimed at the skeleton.

"Jane, double time," Bowen ordered.

She followed David. Bowen took aim.

"*Altares*, we're withdrawing to Kite 1," Bowen said.

"Understood, Tom," Masters said.

Bowen backed away, putting another meter between himself and the hybrid device. Bowen's radio receivers, tuned not only to the light ship but also his surroundings, picked up the hum, which slithered through the air, so unfamiliar a sound that he instantly sensed its other-ness. Following was a cascading tick—the cadence of metal knuckles wrapping against the gangway, finding purchase, steadying.

He turned toward Jane and David. They had reached the system of rungs leading up to ground level. Bowen started toward them. Sound and movement stirred at his back.

Bowen spun around in time to see the Ret machine rise up from the catwalk. It moved with a grace he hadn't dreamed possible, given its age. It stood on what passed for legs, Bowen's height and half more above that, its reticulated metal skeleton flexing, aligning. The motion reminded Bowen of something glimpsed in old video footage in school—a cobra, readying to strike. The Ret machine hummed, waited.

"Dad," David called.

At that moment, all four of the Ret's eyes unsealed, snapping open. The thing turned toward the sound of David's voice. Four cold blue lights beamed in his son's direction.

"No," Bowen barked.

He raised his boom rifle. The Ret monstrosity again focused on him. Bowen saw the protrusions tick, their aim awkward. A flash of blue energy crackled out of one and struck the gantry post less than a meter from where Bowen stood. Acrid smoke wafted up from metal slag.

Its aim was off, but the awakened predator soon compensated. Two of the weapons homed in on Bowen. He gripped the boom stick's trigger. Something tore past Bowen, seen before heard. The discharge struck the Ret's face, knocking it over backward. The sound caught up, an enormous thunderclap that clawed at Bowen's ears over the horn and echoed over and again throughout the dead city's vast underground complex.

Bowen tipped a look behind him. Jane stood with her boom rifle drawn. David had his weapon out of its holster and at the ready.

"Excellent job," Bowen said.

The victory was short-lived. The Ret surged back up, smoke pouring from two if its shattered mechanical eyes. The predator had been injured, and was now even more deadly.

It surged toward them and took aim.

Chapter Fifteen

Information was transmitted over the horn—data on the planet's atmosphere, surface conditions, magnetosphere, weather patterns, and suitability. *Altares'* main computer stored the information as part of the mission's growing collection of amassed knowledge pertaining to its directive.

As Masters called into the radio, "Jane, *fire*," the secondary computer—a backup system designed to support the main frame—ferried the latest updates from the planet, including the ground team's discovery of active alien tech, through a third intermediary, past two additional safety protocols, and into the non-networked unit housed three decks below.

And something asleep in Subcompartment D began to wake up.

The Ret device righted, its two remaining lenses shifting between three armed targets.

"The deck," Bowen shouted. "Aim for the floor beneath it!"

His order didn't require further explanation. Both Jane and David followed Bowen's lead and took aim down at the metal catwalk where the alien horror stood. Bowen fired. Two additional photon discharges sailed after his, blasting into and through the brittle gangway. The Ret reared up, off balance. Thunder again boomed through the under-city, this time at triple the amplitude.

The Ret flailed. Time-weakened metal separated. Then it was falling, firing blindly as it dropped. Long seconds later, the impact bellowed up from the depths of the abyss.

"Let's return to the Kite," Bowen said. "Quickly."

David holstered his side arm and jumped up on the first rung. When he was on his way, Jane followed. Bowen swept the remains of the catwalk with his rifle.

"Tom, do you read us?"

Bowen backed toward the rungs. "I read you, *Altares*."

"What's your situation?"

"Everyone's fine — we're on our way back to the Kite, Skipper."

He heard Masters' sigh of relief over the horn and looked past his left shoulder. Jane was on her way up. An icy sensation slithered over Bowen's epidermis. Shouldering the boom rifle, he hastened over to the rungs and began to climb.

Power fluctuated.

Sensors that had been designed to mask readings in that section of the light ship worked to conceal the extra usage of energy drawn from generators and reserves when required. Most instances escaped notice. Subcompartment D was a streamlined nexus of power distribution junctions connecting to the upper deck and the Photon Drive.

"We're tracking you, ground team," Anna Bowen said over the horn. "And the Ret machine as well. It's four levels below you."

"Is it still activated?" Bowen asked.

"Affirmative. It's on the move."

"Direction?"

"Heading away from you and the Kite."

Power, most of it derived from the light of stars far from the mother planet's, fed into the systems secreted halfway down Subcompartment D. The computer housed in that part of *Altares* made final calculations.

A computer screen activated in the dark of a room walled off from the rest of the light ship. A countdown clock appeared on the monitor, tolling a handful of hours, minutes, and seconds.

2:11:33.

Seconds and minutes began to run out.

Soon, so too would those hours.

"Is it still on your heat trackers, *Altares*?" Bowen asked.

"Yes, Tom. It's moving deeper through the area beneath the city. The thing's fast," Masters said.

Bowen stepped onto the ground-level platform, where David and Jane waited. "Don't we know."

They started back across the ancient complex.

"Why, Dad?" David asked. "Why would their first instinct be to attack us?"

"Especially given that we called down and told them we were friendly," Jane added.

"Maybe our Ret friend didn't hear the message."

They crossed past the division into the city limit and headed toward the exit.

"Do you think it's because the Rets are territorial?" asked Jane. "After all, they've laid claim to this planet."

"But they weren't here first," David said.

"Anyway, the Rets never established a colony here, so even if we wanted to live on Treasure Island, we'd have every right."

"Perhaps they don't see it that way," said Bowen.

They advanced on the exit. The bulk of the city was at their backs, and Bowen was grateful.

"We are moving forward, correct?" David asked. "On to our next surface objective?"

Bowen glanced at his son. David's expression through the atmosuit's helmet was one of concern. The look, Bowen realized, had little to do with the dangers they'd faced and survived, and owed completely to the boy's worry that he'd order the visit to the planet cut short.

"Haven't you had enough of exploring Treasure Island?"

"No," David said.

Bowen inhaled. He was tired and on edge, but his son's enthusiasm drew a smile. "What say you, Jane?"

Jane hesitated from answering.

"Jane?"

The girl looked up at him. "My mother was a painter. Before we knew you."

Bowen was familiar with the end of the story, but not many of the details of Sylvia Masters' life before the families trained for the *Altares* mission. "Oh?"

"Landscapes, mostly. We lived for a

summer on Rankine Lane. My mother loved to paint flowers." The girl again got quiet as they marched the remaining distance to the Kite. At the hatch, Jane faced Bowen. "I'd like to see the flowers."

Bowen sat in the copilot's seat. "Do you still have a track on that Ret device's heat signal, *Altares*?"

"Hold tight a moment, ground team," Anna answered.

Bowen exchanged a look with Jane. As the seconds dragged on, his concern deepened.

"*Altares*, come in," Bowen said.

"We're here, Tom," Masters answered.

"Is everything all right up there?"

"A damn strange thing. We've got power fluctuations in the subcompartment. We're trying to lock down the source of the drain, but…"

"But?"

"It's like the instruments don't want to cooperate. Like they're intentionally feeding us false information."

Bowen glanced out the space window at the vast alien structure, now looking ominous as the sun slipped below its tallest spire. "Where do the fluctuations originate?"

"Subcompartment D," Masters said.

"We recently repaired a similar problem down there."

"Yeah, we're beginning to think one's related to the other. As for the Ret device, it just vanished from our screens, which means it either ran out of power or your shots finally did it in."

"Or that it vanished deeper beneath the surface and beyond our range to track it," Bowen sighed.

He processed the information. They had little over an hour until daylight waned, according to the sun's position in the sky. Enough for a quick look, at least at the flower fields.

"We're readying to leave this location for our second objective," Bowen said. "Unless you need us up there to help resolve the power issues."

"What we're seeing up here is more confounding than catastrophic," Masters said. "Be careful and check in once you reach your next target."

"Will do, Skipper."

Bowen turned to Jane. "Pilot, take us out."

"Yes, sir," Jane said.

She ran through her pre-flight checklist. Weapons were stowed, harnesses secured. Kite 1 engaged her vertical thrusters, ascended up from the dry riverbed, and soared away from the dead city.

He again called up the light ship's schematics on the chart table's screen. The blueprints for Subcompartment D showed nothing but solid bulkhead and circuitry where Anna had indicated storage space. That the odd fluctuations in power and the ship's computer's seeming inability to resolve or identify them both centered on that section of *Altares'* lowest deck made him more inclined to believe her claim.

The Neptune mission. Masters scanned the timestamp on the blueprints. One month after Neptune, and two weeks before *Altares'* launch from Delta Station. He accessed earlier files, six months prior to Neptune. They matched the other schematics. Neither showed storage space in Subcompartment D.

Masters stood from the chart table. The Navigation Area's wall space was a mix of computer systems and physical star charts depicting sections of a galaxy far behind them. Other maps were stored as scrolls in a holder. Masters riffled through the selections, growing more frustrated with each flip.

Anna entered from the Monitoring Area. "Harry?"

"Help me, Anna."

She crossed to the map holder. "What are we looking for?"

He flipped ahead, only to stop and scroll back. "I think I've found it."

Masters pulled out the roll of blueprints

and carried it over to the chart table. He laid it out. The blueprints were physical schematics of *Altares*.

He zeroed in on the lowest deck. Anna followed his pointer finger to the cutaway of Subcompartment D.

"It's true," Masters said. "There's a room hidden down there."

Chapter Sixteen

Crimson spread around the crater walls, a living sea of deep red glowing in the last of the daylight.

"They're beautiful," Jane said. "Hard to believe that they were planted by the same hands that created that machine."

Bowen nodded. "We still lack all the answers, Jane."

The Kite continued to follow the coast. Sunlight dappled the waters. Without a moon to influence tides, Treasure Island's ocean remained placid. While handling the controls, Jane thought back to a day from her childhood spent near the sea. A visit to Grand Metropolis, a city far from home in England. Her mother had been there, and Jane remembered Sylvia Masters laughing as a sudden gust of wind attempted to carry them all away.

Jane smiled. She looked up from the

Kite's instruments at the gentle blue expanse running all the way to the horizon. In a way, Sylvia Masters had traveled with them aboard *Altares*. Even if only through memory, the notion pleased Jane. Her mother would have loved seeing the rolling fields of alien flowers, especially given their range. Flowers on Earth had become rare apart from hot houses and botanical research gardens leading up to the light ship's launch.

David shuffled in behind them. "Two o'clock," the boy said.

"Huh?" asked Jane.

David aimed a gloved finger toward the sky. Jane followed. It was still blue up there, but edging toward the gray of dusk. Beyond her helmet's shield and the Kite's space window, Jane made out the vague shape of the *Altares*, aglow as a result of her running lights. The spacecraft had assumed a stationary orbit in readiness should the ground team need assistance. As exciting as it was exploring the alien planet, Jane knew the light ship was home. She smiled, reassured by *Altares'* closeness.

"We know where we're going," said Bowen. "But do we have our next stop figured out?"

He'd meant the question for his fellow navigator, however it was their pilot who answered.

"Yes," said Jane. "Two o'clock."

She wasn't pointing at the sky now. Her

direction indicated down, toward the necklace of crimson flower fields spilling over impact crater walls.

Bowen switched on the Kite's camera. The image appeared on the screen.

"David," Bowen said.

"On it, Dad."

David moved back into the passenger section, tablet in hand. Jane circled the new point of interest as David tapped at buttons and information streamed in.

"*Altares*," Bowen said.

"Go ahead, Tom," Masters answered.

"We seem to have located one of the three missing support craft from the abandoned alien ship."

On the screen, a perfectly round object filled the center of the impact crater below Kite 1. The crimson flora climbed over two-thirds of the craft's hull, which gleamed dully in the late afternoon sun.

"No active power source," David reported.

"Check for movement—I'd like to avoid another run-in with a Ret machine."

David scanned the surrounding terrain. "I'm not reading any activity down there."

Bowen studied the image on the screen. Like the city, he sensed he was looking at a dead and inert place apart from the lush flora. But he'd been wrong about the city.

"*Altares*, what's your status?"

"We're holding above you, no problems apart from a mystery that's long overdue for solving."

"Why don't you bring us up to speed, Skipper?"

Jane banked the Kite for another pass.

"Harry?"

Masters told them about Anna's certainty that the lowest deck contained a storage area now walled off—something covered up by the computer's schematics, but clearly visible on earlier printout copies of the light ship's blueprints.

"All of the power fluctuations we've experienced are centered around whatever's behind that wall, Tom."

"I find it hard to believe that the Space Authority would send us out here having planted equipment aboard without our knowledge of it."

"There's one more thing, Tom," Anna said.

He sensed the worry in her voice. "Go on, Anna."

"Jim Forbes. He was down in D,' she said. "Only for a few seconds, while I was conducting repairs nine days ago. I think it was part of a message, that it got triggered when I was fixing the system."

"Forbes?"

"Yes, Tom."

"Are you sure you don't want us back

there with you to help sort out things?"

"Finish your look at the planet," Masters said. "I'm about to do the same down in Subcompartment D."

"Roger, *Altares.*" Bowen turned to Jane. "Pick your spot and set us down."

Jane selected a flat area of bare terrain southeast of the alien craft and turned the Kite toward it. Bowen thought of Anna and Forbes. What had happened between them took place far from their present location and was long ended. Still, the sting rose fresh inside him. As Jane made their final approach and David remained vigilant for signs of danger, Bowen considered how seeing Delta Station's commander, even in signal form, must have affected his wife.

Bowen blinked. They were level with the alien escape craft and descending lower for another flawless touchdown. The vessel was circular, mirroring the shape of its mother ship, and listing slightly to one side. The dull metal was mostly covered in festoons of the crimson flowers, which dropped suspending networks of vines, confirming his theory about their flourishing in an environment devoid of pollinating insects.

He stood and moved into the passenger area.

"Still quiet out there," David said.

"Let's hope it remains that way. At the first sign of movement by any Ret tech—or anything else—you're both to return to the Kite, no arguments."

"Understood," Jane said.

David nodded in agreement.

Bowen cycled the hatch open. A temperate breeze billowed in. He wondered if the air was sweet from the flowers. Their vibrant color extended from the alien escape craft all the way up and beyond the crater wall.

Like a red carpet rolled out just for us, thought Bowen.

He hefted the weight of his boom rifle from one gloved hand to the other and stepped onto the ground. The soil here was thicker, likely held together and protected from erosion by root networks running beneath the surface. Unlike the terrain surrounding the city, few stones were obvious, and none of them the size of those in the dry riverbed.

Cultivation, Bowen thought. It was feasible that the entire necklace of impact craters had been selected for the Ret's saw-tooth flowers because of nutrients and minerals released by the pulverizing forces of space debris crashing into the planet's surface.

The flowers themselves were impressive, each blossom twice the size of his hand. The texture looked like velvet or some approximation of sponge. They also appeared to be an alien variant of an evergreen, as few of the blooms surrounding them and the alien spaceship were past prime.

"They're beautiful," Jane said.

David scanned the flower fields. "If the city was an attempt at terraforming the planet, these plants have maintained the atmosphere's breathability. They're producing the perfect amount of oxygen."

"So it's safe to assume that the Rets had similar air needs to our own," Jane said.

"It would appear so, yes."

Bowen marched over the bare soil leading up to the exposed face of the alien craft. The ship was, he guessed, at least five times the width of the Kite, and easily the same in height. There were no visible space windows or airlocks from his angle of approach.

"Two alien races," Bowen sighed. "Two attempts to terraform this planet."

He looked higher. The first star was visible overhead. Its glow was steady, though didn't twinkle as was the nature of stars when their light greeted atmosphere. He realized it was the *Altares*, still overhead and holding watch while other stars were in hiding.

Anna thumbed the intercom. "Harry?"

Masters exited the elevator. He approached the wall terminal and responded. "Go ahead, Anna."

"I've found it. A program buried so deep in encryption that no one would ever have known it was there without these power fluctuations to give it away. It's listed as 'the Daughter Initiative'."

Masters absorbed the information. "Daughter Initiative? Does that mean anything to you? Or anything Forbes discussed on Delta?"

"No," Anna said.

"Well, I'm here. I'll let you know if I find anything."

"Good hunting, Harry," Anna said.

Masters faced Subcompartment D before starting down the long corridor.

O:O:11

Chapter Seventeen

Forbes sat at his desk, looking stately and confident in his white Space Authority uniform with its black collar and sleeve stripes. He was a man used to getting his way, though in this instance he'd been overruled from higher up the chain of command.

The woman seated on the other side of the big desk noted the commander's smile, and also understood that it was a façade, a necessary defense that the man in charge of Delta Station had practiced to perfection.

"For the record, Shervin—is that *Miss* Shervin, or do you prefer that I use your first name?"

"Shervin will do, Commander."

"For the record, I'm completely opposed to this plan."

"So noted," she said. "Though it doesn't

change the situation. Any grievances on your behalf should be taken up with the Earth Authority, not me."

Forbes' smile widened. He chuckled once, another of his practiced responses, Shervin guessed. "Are you suggesting I should file an official complaint form? On a mission that won't even be acknowledged, at least not by the Earth Authority?"

"What is it you'd like from me, Commander Forbes?"

Forbes studied her—not in the way Shervin had noticed him look at the crew's doctor, Anna Bowen. The nuances were so subtle as to be barely recognizable, but little escaped Shervin's power of observation.

"Your word," he said.

"I don't answer to the Space Authority."

Forbes' smile dropped, and Shervin saw the man's true face, and it was easy to believe that the feelings he held for Anna Bowen were legitimate, if secret. "In this one case, you do."

Shervin leaned back as far as the chair permitted. How many dignitaries had sat where she was? Leaders from both the Earth and Space Authorities, religious figures, heads of state visiting Delta Station and, likely, Anna Bowen on numerous occasions. Shervin, too, had acquired a mask after ten years of service. She flashed a confident response, though inside she acknowledged her first jolt of worry. Forbes was diplomatic, and the Earth Authority had his cooperation at this point, but that could change. He was a man in power to be respected and, perhaps, feared.

"I'm listening, Commander."

"No matter what happens, no matter how far you travel, you're not to hurt them. Ever. Do you understand me?"

Shervin's smile dropped in response. "I can give you my word that it isn't my intention to want to hurt the crew of *Allures*."

"That's no answer. It's not the one I need."

"It's the best I can offer."

Forbes leaned back. His eyes never left her. "What will you do if they stop at Alpha Centauri? Proxima Centauri b, the only planet in the system, is a rock ravaged by stellar winds 2,000 times greater than those that hit the Earth."

She started to answer. "We'll—"

"What does that do to your Daughter Initiative?"

"If the crew calls it quits in Alpha Centauri, we come home to Earth with them, and none will be the wiser."

"A second crew," Forbes sighed. "I don't like it."

"So you've stated."

"And let me reiterate—you have your mission, sanctioned by the Earth Authority. I have mine, which is first and foremost the safety of the Masters and Bowen families. Don't harm them. *Please*."

It was Forbes' final word that affected her more than all the others that preceded it. For weeks, she, like most of Earth, the lunar cities, and those on Delta and at work constructing Epsilon Station, had watched the five crewmembers of *Altares* get paraded in front of cameras, their mission hailed as carrying the hopes of the planet with it. Only a handful of the hopeful knew about the clandestine, second mission associated with the launch. Shervin's team would never get the same fanfare or accolades as Harry Masters or Forbes' precious Anna Bowen and, yes, a good part of her silently regretted the disparity. Now, the *Altares* crew was human more than heroes or icons, because the man on the other side of the desk cared about them. Her especially.

"We're all on the same side," she said.

"Are we?"

Forbes began to fade. His office on Space Station Delta dissolved. Everything transferred into snowy specks drifting across a black backdrop.

The Universe, Shervin thought.

Then pain raced up from her core, shocking her out of her slumber. Her eyes shot open. At first, there was only darkness and confusion. She was dead, likely for a long while. The *Altares* mission had failed. The ship was destroyed, burned up, her particles scattered across the space between stars.

But the exquisite misery persisted, proof

of life.

She sucked down a breath. The air was cool and had a chemical edge. No, she was alive. Now, the only question that mattered was where were they — back in orbit around Earth, docked to either Delta or Epsilon Station, or in deep space?

Had they reached their mission objective?

Shervin came out of the fog. The unit's cover loomed directly over her face. Her exhale condensed on the transparency, and her next response was panic. It hadn't released automatically. She was going to suffocate.

Then her training kicked in. Shervin located the manual release and gripped it with her right hand. A firm tug yielded no results. She pulled again. This time, the lid detached. Automated systems took over, pulling the cover around the cryogenic coffin. A light flickered overhead and then stabilized. Its glow reestablished the boundaries of the room: four coffins in all, and a wall of priceless instrumentation panels attached to power systems, backups, and additional feeds twice that number.

Shervin sat up. The confines of the surrounding world did a spin. Ceiling and floor attempted to exchange places. She focused. Blood flowed. Muscles thawed. On her next attempt, the universe stabilized.

Warm air gusted over her, vented from a unit above her cryogenic bed. The sleep suit she'd gone under in now fit with an awkwardness, like a layer of dead skin. Despite the heat pouring down, her teeth began to chatter. She willed them to stop. They obeyed.

Shervin kicked her legs over the edge of the coffin. Her bare soles connected with the deck. Chills raced up through her flesh. *Altares*. The light ship was intact. Her location and the number of years since leaving Delta Station on the head of a comet's photon trail were mysteries that would have to endure for another few necessary minutes.

She checked Latham's coffin. His wakeup call was initiated, Tasser's to follow, and Gouldian's last, as planned. Staggering them out was less likely to draw attention to the incredible power needs required to end their sleep and activate each unit. Shervin moved over to the locker situated between the instrument panels. A fresh Earth Authority uniform hung among the others with her name on it. Her holdall contained undergarments. One new pair of boots in her size was among the four waiting on the locker's floor.

Shervin removed the sleep suit, grateful to have it off her, and dressed. By the time she was lacing her right boot, Latham's unit powered fully down, and the heat vent above his sleep coffin billowed warm air in readiness for his emerging.

She released the lid. Latham looked around.

"Shervin?" he asked.

She extended her hand. He took it, his grip strong, a good sign.

"Do you know where we are yet?"

She shook her head. "Come and help me."

Shervin assisted him up. Latham glanced around and then exited the coffin. He dressed. Tasser's sleep cycle ended. They greeted the other male in their team of four.

"That only leaves Lady Gouldian," Tasser said.

"Welcome her back," Shervin said. "While I try to figure out where—and when—we are."

The men dressed in their Earth Authority uniforms. Shervin activated the computer terminal on the section of wall containing their instruments and keyed in her security code. The monitor lit, showing the curve of a blue planet as glimpsed from beneath one of the light ship's wings.

"By our Mother," Shervin sighed. "We're in orbit around a planet."

Latham moved beside her. "Is that an ocean?"

"So it would appear. And a significant one, I'd say, given the view."

"A welcome sight," said Latham.

Shervin agreed, but refused to allow herself to indulge in a smile. "Let's not forget why we're here. Tasser, stay with Gouldian.

Latham, help me assess the equipment. We need to know that everything else made the journey with us, or none of this matters."

Latham nodded. Together, they checked the four panels.

"How's it look?" Tasser asked.

Now, Shervin permitted a smile. "It's all intact and viable. We did it."

Gouldian's coffin lid released. Tasser took the woman's hand. "Lady Gouldian. Welcome back."

She twisted Tasser's hand. Laughing, he surrendered.

"Fine, you win!"

"My thought exactly," Latham said. "We won."

Shervin wanted to caution him from claiming victory so soon. But before she could, the wall at her left separated into four triangular wedges. The pieces drew back into bulkhead. Light from the corridor outside spilled in, and a lone figure clad in a white and blue Space Authority uniform stood beyond the secret door, looking in.

"What in hell-?" Harry Masters said.

Chapter Eighteen

The only fenestration in the seamless metal of the alien craft's hull came in the form of four sets of doors, oval like the hatches discovered on the mother ship. One of the doors stood open, barely visible beneath an overhanging canopy of crimson flowers. As Bowen approached, his mind filled in details. According to their design, all four of the hatches could be exposed for loading or offloading cargo, or to aid in the quick evacuation of crew.

He nudged aside the flora. Daylight crept into the circular realm beyond, dispelling shadows.

"Look sharp, Tom," Anna said over the horn.

Bowen smiled. "I promise, sweetheart."

He thought of her up there, in the Navigation Area, watching the ground team's progress through the electronic eyes gazing out from his helmet, also there and connected to him via the radio. Whatever the nature of the mysteries that had his wife seeing visions of Jim Forbes, Bowen knew he and Anna were good again.

Bowen stepped past the hatch and onto solid footing. He activated the helmet's lights. Twin beams strobed out and into the center of the craft. The layout was a version of a figure eight. He stood in the bottom loop. The top waited beyond another open, oval hatch. Grooves similar to those seen in the mother ship's landing bay streaked the walls. The way ahead brooded in darkness.

"Dad," David called.

Bowen turned back. "What is it, son?"

"Look."

Bowen followed David's lead. Both he and Jane were still outside, their focus aimed away from the alien craft, in the direction of the flower fields.

"What do you think it is?" asked Jane.

Bowen wasn't sure what he was looking at. The curiosity that held their attention was a series of markers, each in the rudimentary form of the letter 'V', jutting up from the bed of flowers. Bowen counted seventeen. The markers resembled the same material from which the craft's hull was constructed. Some of the seventeen stood straight up from the field of crimson petals. Others had bent over time. Given the age of the craft, it was possible that more had been raised only to topple, or had been dragged down beneath the flowers.

The layout activated a memory from Earth, something he'd seen in a photograph from another time when human society buried their dead in the soil.

"It's a graveyard," Bowen said, his voice barely above a whisper.

Anna stood at the chart table, her entire body tense. With Harry investigating Subcompartment D and the rest of the crew down on the planet, the sense that she was the last living being in the universe crept around her, offering an unwanted embrace.

Below, night inched over the planet. She tipped her eyes toward the porthole. The curve of Treasure Island was already dark.

"Come home," she whispered.

Of course, leaving the surface early would mean a waste of resources and time. They were already down there and had located one of the missing pieces of a larger puzzle. It was the ground team's duty to follow through. But when the Kite was on its way up from the surface, she'd look forward to the night's sleep that was promised, with all members of the *Altares* mission safely returned home.

Home. That word resonated in her thoughts. She supposed anywhere that Tom,

David, and she were together qualified. She'd felt that way at Beta Spaceport and the succession of university apartments before assignment to the light ship. But the word had expanded, because their family had grown by two, and now home meant Harry and Jane Masters as well.

The chill encompassing her flesh deepened. Anna pulled her uniform jacket tighter and drew up the zipper. The cold was an omen, and in evidence of some threat to home and family that manifested in the seconds that followed.

The chart table sang out a mechanical note in warning. Anna came out of her thoughts and took her husband's empty seat. *Altares'* eyes-in-the-skies had detected an unusual reading below. Those scanners not committed to watching the light ship's proximity for the approach of space debris were focused on the ground team's location.

Anna tapped the button flashing on the console. The live camera feed from her husband's helmet reduced in size. The screen flashed words: Multiple Power Sources Detected.

Her pulse quickened. Anna stabbed at buttons. The screen altered again, becoming a view of the surface as seen from *Altares'* eyes — desert terrain edged in crimson.

"Overlay," she said aloud, the sound of her voice coming twice as loud in the cavernous silence of the light ship's top deck.

The computer assigned shape and color to the readings—sidewinding snakes of pale blue color, at least a dozen, moving in formation across the overlaid grid. For a second, she considered it might be seismic activity, a mistake on the warning system's part. An earthquake would be dangerous enough, though she understood the snake-like movements for what they truly were.

She zoomed in the surface picture. Along the dividing line between crimson flora and impact crater soil, Anna clearly made out the round mass of the alien craft and the cleaner angles of Kite 1.

"My God," Anna gasped. She thumbed the radio. "Tom!"

"Go ahead," Bowen said.

"Ship's scanners have detected a dozen powered contacts all converging on your present location. Get out of there now!"

"Roger that, *Altares*."

Bowen turned away from the alien cemetery. Sunlight rained down at an angle, illuminating the flowers and burnishing their petals in the day's dying glow that, on a quick glance, liquefied them to the eye, transforming them into an expanse of spilled blood.

"You're positive?" he called up to the ship.

"The patterns match those of the Ret mechanism you encountered in the city."

Bowen scanned the horizon. Shadows spilled down from the crater wall. Nothing else moved. "We're on our way home, *Altares*." Then, to the others, he barked, "Jane, David, return to the Kite. We've got visitors!"

Jane raised her rifle and marched forward. David didn't straggle. It was an efficient evacuation, thought Bowen. Exactly what he expected from his ground team.

"Jane, you'll need to skip your pre-flight checklist," he said. "I want us airborne immediately."

"Yes, sir," Jane said.

The Kite was before them, its pilot's space window and passenger's portholes aglow in the dying sunlight. Bowen risked a smile, and a moment later paid for it as the ground gave out beneath his boots, and the world around him went blurry with confusion.

Pain raced up his right leg. When he could focus again, Bowen found himself standing in a sinkhole up past his waist. Another of the V-shaped markers jutted out of the ground, mostly hidden by saw-tooth petals the color of human blood.

He'd fallen into the remains of an alien grave, he saw in the instant of clarity that followed. The crunch of bones beneath his boots was unmistakable, as was the source of his pain. One of those rib bones from the reticulated skeleton had sliced through his atmosuit material, which was dense enough to resist even a direct shot from a boom stick.

His cries brought the others back. They appeared at the edge of the collapsed grave. Jane reached down.

"Take my hand," she said.

Bowen did. He shifted forward, only to recoil. Looking down, he saw that he was still impaled upon the alien skeleton. The misery in his leg surged.

"*Tom*," Anna called. "You've got to get off the surface now—they're almost on top of you!"

"We've got a problem, *Altares*," David said.

Then, without hesitation, David jumped down into the depression and located the issue.

"It doesn't look deep," David said. "But your atmosuit's been compromised, and we need to get you out of here."

"I'm ready," Bowen said.

David gripped the impalement. Bowen steadied himself, and Jane pulled. Bowen trapped the scream behind clenched teeth and powered out of the depression. He could suffer the pain once he was back in his wife's medical domain.

They hastened in the direction of Kite 1, with Bowen leaning on David, the two acting out a desperate version of a three-legged race. Two-dozen meters from their destination, the

Kite lurched. Plumes of dirt and rock exploded up from the ground in a crude circle around the spacecraft. Following came streamers of hot blue energy that severed the Kite's wings and sliced through hull, avionics, and engine.

Kite 1 came apart in a spectacular detonation that sent smoke, flame, and shrapnel up into the twilight sky, and knocked the three members of the ground team off their feet.

Chapter Nineteen

Masters followed the length of corridor down through Subcompartment D to the place on the schematics where he'd seen the storage area. The wall appeared solid apart from the computer terminal where Anna had encountered the specter of Jim Forbes.

He pondered the story. A recording or holographic image made sense—something triggered by the ebb and surge of power through that section of the ship. But why would Jim Forbes make such a message and then keep it secret? There should not have been anything restricted from the crew by their superiors.

Masters felt along the grooves. The first of four cuts passed beneath his fingertips, each joining together like the airlocks in other sections of the light ship. A hatch! Behind it was the storage room, and whatever secrets Forbes and the Space Authority had hidden from crew and captain.

He located the release and pulled. The hatch separated into four uniform quarters and pulled into the surrounding wall. Masters stood looking at the storage space on the original blueprints, and what it contained.

The room was approximately the size of the Flight Deck. It contained four beds—the kind used for deep space missions before *Altares* and the development of the Martin B Photon Drive Engine.

Cryogenic coffins, he thought.

There were instruments—four panels feeding off the ship's power. The sleep beds alone had likely devoured an enormous amount of *Altares'* energy output, and no doubt were behind the fluctuations. But the Space Authority had worked hard to keep this part of the ship hidden from them, and those beds had already released three of their occupants.

The woman and two men standing on the other side of the secret entrance wore versions of Earth Authority uniforms, body-conscious and military in design. The room's fourth occupant, a second woman, looked newly awakened and was still in the process of leaving her cryogenic bed.

"What in hell-?" Masters gasped.

For the next moment, he considered that he, too, was seeing ghosts on the light ship's lowest deck. The four humans hidden behind the wall were holograms, or figments of his tired mind.

But he quickly understood that the quartet was real, as was the threat they posed. The Earth Authority, the Space program's partner in all human affairs, had infiltrated his ship. A quick glance made it clear that the two men and women were soldiers. It was more than their physical magnificence, the cut of their hair, or their uniforms. No, it was in their eyes, now aimed at him in shock that was soon to pass.

Masters turned and raced back up the corridor, the weapons locker outside the starboard hangar his destination. Boots pounded on the floor behind him. At the bend in the corridor, he saw the taller of the two men in pursuit.

"*Stop!*" the man shouted.

Masters didn't. This was his ship. He gave the orders.

His pursuer caught up and grabbed hold of his shoulder just shy of the locker. Masters planted his right foot, pivoted, and drove his fist into the man's stomach. The move was effective. The soldier fell. As he did, Masters saw another moving behind him, the first woman in that uniform from another time and place long since gone. He noticed the patch on the arm of her shirt first—something that resembled a woman and child. The child was female.

Daughter, Masters thought. *The Daughter Initiative.*

Then he saw that she was armed.

"No," Masters said.

The woman fired.

The world around him vanished in an effulgence of blinding white light before going dark as an eclipse fell over his senses.

They were with General Bishop again — Masters, Jane, and the Bowens. Bishop was giving another of his famous speeches designed to boost their emotions. You couldn't help but be motivated when in the general's company.

"And our galaxy — one among millions of galaxies strewn throughout the infinity of space — in a universe not only stranger than we imagine, but stranger than we can imagine."

He liked Bishop, with his platinum hair and pale blue eyes, and how, though a seasoned man of space, the general still approached exploration with the enthusiasm of the young.

"The light ship *Altares*," Bishop continued. "The first of its kind to harness the limitless power of the photon..."

Masters recalled the speech, one of the general's more memorable performances. He reached for Jane, as he'd done then during the original delivery. But his daughter was gone. In her place stood the woman with neat, dark hair and chocolate eyes that'd stunned him in the corridor outside the starboard hangar.

"This is all about second chances," said a

different man. Masters recognized him. It was Jim Forbes. "Though you board *Altares* against my wishes, you take our hopes with you beyond Mother Earth's shore."

Masters looked around. The Bowens were gone, replaced by three intruders dressed in Earth Authority uniforms. General Bishop, too. In his stead stood Forbes in his crisp white and black Delta Station colors.

"Good luck, and pray you succeed in your mission," Forbes said. And then he winked out, as he had in the corridor in Anna's report of their earlier encounter.

Masters tracked a residue of light over to one of the wall panels. A holographic recording. Anna *had* unburied part of the message during her repairs to the power system in the subcompartment. A secret plan involving Forbes—according to his words, he wasn't keen on whatever reason had led to the Earth Authority smuggling four stowaways aboard his command. But Forbes had caved in the end.

"He's awake," the taller of the two men said.

Masters was on one of the vacated cryogenic beds. He started to rise, only to find himself flanked by the taller man and the second woman who'd occupied the bed at the moment of his discovery. Both were armed.

The woman who'd stunned him approached, her face beautiful but hard around the edges.

"Who are you?" Masters demanded.

The woman faced him directly. Masters knew she was in charge of the Earth Authority team by the way she didn't blink. As the last of the fog lifted and his body woke from being stunned by a boom stick on its lowest setting, Masters greeted the woman's eyes, determined to not divert first. He succeeded.

"I'm Shervin," she said. "That's Latham, Tasser, and Gouldian."

"You're Earth Authority?"

"Clearly."

Masters flashed a cocky smirk. "Hate to break it to you, but if you hadn't noticed, you're on a Space Authority vessel."

Shervin matched his expression. "We know full well where we are—the celebrated light ship *Altares*, Captain Masters."

Masters' grin widened. "So you're aware that by assaulting me, you've broken a number of laws that officials on both sides of the aisle would frown upon."

"File a complaint, Captain," Shervin said coolly.

"We're a long way from home for that, if you haven't guessed."

Shervin turned and looked at the computer screen, now showing *Altares*' camera view of the planet's curve as it surrendered to nightfall. "We're closer to home than you think."

Masters cast a glance at the screen before returning to Shervin. "Why are you and your team on my ship?"

She straightened, folded her arms.

"Should I file a complaint with the Earth Authority about that matter, too? Do you realize exactly how far we've traveled since setting out from Earth?"

Shervin said, "We know all of it, Captain. After waking up, we reviewed your progress—Alpha Centauri first, the malfunction of the Photon Drive that sent you out of control into the heart of our former galaxy, and your journey through the black hole to this universe, this orbit around the blue planet."

"Then you know we can never go home," Masters said. "If your plan is to seize control of the *Altares* for the Earth Authority, you're on a fool's errand."

Shervin laughed. "Our errand was never to return to Earth. Our mission objective is right here, Captain. We have arrived."

"To the Daughter," said Gouldian.

"Bless the Daughter," the man called Tasser said.

"Amen," Latham finished.

Masters absorbed the information, his smile dropping. "What exactly is your mission?"

Shervin leaned down. Again, they were face-to-face, this time closer. "That world out there that you and your crew discovered, we intend to claim it."

"It's already been claimed—twice."

"Then the third time's the charm,"

Shervin said. "That blue planet beneath us and *Altares*...Captain Masters, you're looking at the new home of the human race. And pity anyone who tries to stop us from completing our mission."

Chapter Twenty

"Kite 1, do you hear me?" Anna called into the horn. "*Tom.*"

Only static answered. Maintaining a calm façade, Anna checked the system. *Altares* was broadcasting at optimum. The connection had been severed on the ground. Panic crept in and attempted to possess her. She exorcized it, focused the scanners, and saw the remains of the explosion where the Kite had been seconds before, displayed as a waning heat signature among the coils indicating the Ret machines.

"No," Anna gasped.

A coldness filled her. Jane, Tom, and David…

Anna shook her head, banishing the thought. Even as tears pooled in her eyes, making it difficult to see clearly, her hands continued to work the controls. The screen expanded, and the scanners obeyed. There, beyond the cooling bloom of heat and debris, were three lesser signatures, located between the destroyed Kite and the alien support craft. *Three*. The horn was down, but the ground team was still alive!

As she watched, the hostile contacts converged. She fast-thumbed buttons on the scanner controls. The Ret mech had traveled beneath the surface and were tunneling their way up from the ground. The proverbial pit of vipers, Anna thought. A dozen contacts. And once they were up there, Tom, Jane, and David wouldn't stand a chance against those numbers.

"Harry, I need you up here immediately," she called into the ship-wide intercom.

He didn't answer, and again Anna suffered the illusion that she was completely alone in this new universe. The certainty grew. Another second and it would paralyze her with the sting of a deep frost. Heat surged. Anna moved along the row of instruments to the laser controls.

Altares boasted two high-impact cannons, fore and aft. Their design was meant to eradicate the danger posed by space debris, but they'd function just as efficiently against this threat, she reasoned. Anna targeted the nest of vipers. The computer shrieked a note, arguing her decision. The forward cannon housed in the directional antenna was unable to lock on, given their orbital position and angle.

"Sorry, Harry," Anna said.

She hastened into the Flight Deck and took the pilot's seat. A two-second jolt from the port steering rockets sent the light ship off her even keel and tipped the directional antenna into perfect alignment with the planet's surface.

She checked the screen. The heat signature from the destroyed Kite winked out completely, leaving all dozen contacts still clustered together. But only for another moment, for they were on the move.

"*Fire*," Anna said, and pushed the trigger on the pilot's instrument panel.

Altares' forward laser cannon responded. A powerful streamer of green energy surged out and down, slicing through the stratosphere and blasting into the planet's surface.

The Kite came apart in a spectacular mushroom of flame and shrapnel. The concussion knocked Bowen off his unsteady legs, taking both of his supporters in the deal. Those Ret mechs hadn't approached from the surface. No, they were moving underground, according to their method of attack. They'd cut beneath the Kite, fired up once they were in position. The Kite was destroyed, and now those same mech were tunneling up to finish the job.

"*Altares*, do you read me?" Bowen called.

The horn crackled in response.

"*Altares!*"

He picked himself up and scrambled for the boom rifle. In the dying conflagration that had been the Kite, the first of multiple sets of unblinking blue eyes appeared, stark beyond the roiling black smoke. There were so many. Too many.

"Retreat to the alien ship," Bowen said. "Hurry!"

Jane started ahead of his son. David held close to Bowen's side, offering assistance.

"Quickly, David—I'll cover you," Bowen said.

The sky erupted in a scream. Bowen turned away as the powerful blast of laser energy streaked down from the light ship and hammered the cluster of Ret mechs. This explosion dwarfed the previous many times over. The ground trembled. Thunder boomed across the dusk landscape. The show of force was beyond effective. Glorious, even.

Well done, sweetheart, Bowen thought, even as the firmament around him quaked, and the new night burned.

Anna held her breath. Instruments set before the pilot's seat updated. The new crater added to Treasure Island's pocked face no longer read power signatures from a dozen Ret death machines. She offered a silent prayer to whatever deity was listening and turned the scanners on the direction of the ground team. To her relief, all three life forms registered. She drew in and expelled a cleansing sip of air.

Altares was still canted to starboard. She activated the steering rockets on that side of the light ship and *Altares* resumed her level footing above the planet.

"Hold on, Tom," she said to the empty Flight Deck. "We're on our way down to collect you and the kids."

She vacated the pilot's seat. Harry — he hadn't answered any of her calls. Surely, he'd noted the drastic change of *Altares'* position and the unmistakable bravado of the laser being fired. So why wasn't he back up on the top deck?

Subcompartment D.

Anna approached the radio and activated the ship's intercom. "Harry, please respond."

She imagined her voice carrying through the ship on a lonely echo. Something more was wrong aboard *Altares* than simple power fluctuations.

"Harry, our families need us," she said.

When he didn't answer following that declaration, she flipped several switches. Internal cameras activated, detailing Subcompartment D. The view down the corridor looked as she expected. Then Anna focused on the section of wall where she knew a storage room had been. An airlock hatch had materialized at the center. She gleaned lights and movement beyond its threshold, but the camera angle denied a clearer view.

Then a woman with close-cropped hair dressed in what looked to be an Earth Authority uniform stepped through the hatch and into the corridor. She carried a case strapped to one shoulder, a box-shaped instrumentation panel whose nature Anna couldn't identify.

Her initial shock passed. Intruders were aboard the *Altares*. As she tracked the woman moving quickly up the corridor, it registered that said intruder could have been there all along, hidden behind the façade of corridor wall.

She switched cameras and tracked the woman to the portside hangar, where another stranger waited at the hatch to Kite 2. He, too, had lugged some form of instrumentation to the airlock. Two intruders. Anna watched them release the airlock and enter the Kite. Lights switched on inside the smaller spaceship. Systems powered up.

"No," Anna said.

Intruders had silenced *Altares*' captain and now looked ready to hijack the only means to rescue the ground team from the planet surface, short of jettisoning the light ship's nosecone for reentry.

She watched, waited. Another glance down the corridor showed the invading force numbered more than two. The intruders inside Kite 2 exited the ship minus their payload. Anna thumbed a switch.

"Computer," she said aloud.

The system responded with a musical

note.

"Voice authorization—Bowen, Anna. Seal the hatch to Kite 2 and lock the port hangar. Do not release except on my order or that of Harry Masters, captain of *Altares*."

The system acknowledged. On the screen, the Kite's airlock pulled back together, forming a solid barrier.

"Hold on a little longer, Tom," she said to the smaller window on the screen, still locked on the planet's night face and the three life signs representing the ground team.

Anna broke focus and marched into the Monitoring Area. She activated the bio-panel. The system had been designed for up-close use. Even so, she knew its limitations. She set it for a ship-wide report. The unit isolated six bio-readings—two identifiable because their signatures were already in the system. Harry was alive!

"Thank heavens," Anna said.

So the intruders numbered four. While reaching beneath the table that supported her high-res microscope and other scanning equipment, she made connections. The Earth Authority had smuggled soldiers onto *Altares*. Those soldiers had likely traveled from Sol asleep inside cryogenic coffins. Those sleep chambers would require a great deal of energy to run, which explained the power fluctuations in the ship's subcompartment.

Had Forbes been in on the deception? Her

ghostly visitation was likely a recorded message, part of which she'd un-bottled during repairs.

Anna located the lockbox and pulled it out of hiding. Forbes no longer mattered. Nor did four Earth Authority Special Forces soldiers when her family needed her.

She keyed in the code. The box unlocked. Anna withdrew the side arm and thumbed off the boom stick's safety.

In the Monitoring Area, she saw numerous figures huddled around the Kite's hatch. Harry was among them, held prisoner by a tall man with a drawn weapon.

A dark-haired woman attempted to access the Kite's sealed hatch. When her second try failed, she turned and faced the camera.

"Stand ready," the woman said.

She vanished from the screen.

Long seconds later, Anna heard the unmistakable sound of the elevator rising up from the subcompartment.

Chapter Twenty-one

A stunned silence fell over the new night. The green glare persisted, burning as an afterimage superimposed on the inside of Bowen's eyelids, there again whenever he blinked.

Altares was up there and watching over them. Help would be coming.

He scrambled back to his feet, aware of his compromised atmosuit in the jolt of pain that rippled outward from his wound. The gouge wasn't particularly deep, but enough of a problem to have left them stranded on Treasure Island, and down by one working Kite.

The other two members of the ground team joined him on their feet.

"Everyone okay?" he asked.

Gone was the background hum that meant he was connected to their radios by the horn. Sighing, he released the magnetic straps holding his helmet in place and removed it. With oxygen tank refills gone along with everything else inside the Kite, including their horn link to *Altares* and one another, it was only a matter of hours before the others would be forced to breathe the planet's atmosphere.

"*Dad,*" David yelled into his helmet's face shield.

Bowen sucked down a deep breath. The air was warm and sweet with the floral scent of alien flowers and a saline note from the ocean, carried east on the desert breeze. Its layers overwhelmed him, the mixture in his lungs nearly intoxicating. The surrounding saw-tooth flora exuded a pleasant fragrance, akin to flowers he recalled from boyhood visits to the botanical gardens and later excursions to the greenhouses and hydroponic centers at Beta Spaceport and Delta Station. There were no harmful viral or bacterial agents present, and the planet's atmosphere was in perfect balance for human requirements.

No, he realized that his body was reacting to its first taste of pure country air in untold years and galactic distances. A smile tempted his lips. In spite of what they'd just survived, the planet's air was a welcome reminder of home, and a reason to be thankful. Kites could be replaced from spare parts and honest sweat. Ground team members could not.

"I'm fine," Bowen said. "It's the freshest

air I've ever known."

He wrapped one arm around David's shoulder, the other around Jane, and turned them away from the smoldering crater and slag.

"What do we do?" Jane asked.

"*Altares* knows where we are, and my guess is they'll soon be on their way down to collect us. Until then, I don't want us hanging around out here in the open, should more of those hacked-off alien machines come searching to settle scores."

They faced the dead alien escape pod, whose dark outline hovered against a night sky thickening with storm clouds. Bowen remembered that they were in the center of an alien graveyard, and shook off thoughts of cursed places and haunted houses on his way back to the fenestration.

Altares' well-timed laser blast had rocked the crater enough to shift the alien craft out of its resting position. Now, more of the crimson blanket had fallen to cover the airlock. Bowen released his two team members, steadied on his own legs, and pulled. The saw-tooth flora was incredibly light in his gloved hand and detached easily, baring the way in.

David activated his helmet's lights. The dual beams reached past the vestibule and into the main chamber. Jane followed suit. They made it to the oval hatch, where the grooves inset into walls curbed, continuing their concentricities into a round inner chamber filled with silent machinery and chairs with tall, cowled metal backs.

David withdrew his tablet and scanned the chamber.

"Anything?" Bowen asked.

"Everything's dead,' David said.

Then the device beeped. David turned it toward one of the seatbacks and slowly approached.

"What is it?"

David eyed his father and then rounded the seat, only to jump back, trapping most of a scream behind his teeth. In that moment, Bowen was reminded that his son was still a boy, in spite of the maturity and skills he so often displayed.

Bowen limped over. In the quivering light beams, he saw the source of David's fright: plastered against the metal chair were the desiccated remains of another Ret, little more than bone with papery tissue stretched across skeleton.

Jane removed her helmet. The light inside the alien escape craft dimmed by half.

"What could be taking them so long?" she asked.

The girl gave voice to what Bowen wondered as minutes dragged past the hour mark. By standard calculations, even following a routine pre-flight checklist and given *Altares'* position overhead, a Kite cutting down through nearly a hundred miles of atmosphere should have been on the ground thirty-odd minutes earlier.

He shook his head. "Unless there are problems up there that we don't know about…"

His memory circled back to the power fluctuations reported in Subcompartment D.

Bowen started back toward the vestibule, and from there to the fenestration. The fragrance of the flowers intensified. He detected a strange tapping cadence, at first unsure of what he was hearing. Rain, Bowen realized.

He looked up. Storm clouds now covered the sky, blotting out the field of crystalline stars and also the running lights holding directly over their location.

The night dragged on, becoming the longest of Bowen's life.

"Dad, sit down and rest," David said.

The boy had removed his atmosuit's helmet. Bowen's was upside down in the garden of saw-tooth flowers, gathering the rain. David noted his father's innovation and made a similar move, positioning his helmet beside Bowen's.

"Just in case," David said.

"We have no rations, and we don't know what's going on up there."

David took his father's arm and guided him back inside to the craft's central chamber.

From there, he led Bowen to one of the empty alien seats. The alignment was miserable against his backbone, not at all like the familiar comfort of his station at the chart table, but Bowen welcomed being off his feet. The hollow cadence of falling rain conspired to seduce him. Soon, against his will, he drifted off.

"We are 'Gardeners', you know," said a voice, one deep in timbre but also full of holes. It was neither male nor female but of a tone that suggested both.

Gardeners?

"Oh, yes—keepers of the sacred *Iodi*. The red flame that grows across home soil. It always traveled with us, no matter how far we went. And it was with us when we were forced through the galactic aperture, to the shores of this world. The Iodi survived, even flourished so far from the world of our ancestors, though so many of my fellow *Khamanduhl* perished following the decision to land."

Bowen found himself drifting in a purple haze. His consciousness was back in the plumes where *Altares* had refueled her chemical rockets. He could almost make out the configuration of the abandoned alien mother ship.

"It was never our intention to die here," the voice continued. "But the heart, the *soul*, of Khamanduhl long for the soil, even when it lies fallow and resists putting forth life."

"It's getting lighter in here," another voice said, obviously female.

"Jane?" Bowen asked the void.

He sensed himself standing. The vision of the gas plumes shorted out, the roiling purple curtains going dark.

"What happened?" Bowen asked. "Did you hear it?"

Both Jane and David stood a few meters away beside a length of alien console.

"Hear what?" David asked.

"The voice," Bowen said, and then felt foolish. A dream, one born of exhaustion, that was all it was. A hallucination. He also considered the possibility that his wound had grown infected, and that he was feverish.

Only Bowen didn't feel shaky or damp, and true to Jane's claim, the alien instrumentation had taken on a faint glow. He tracked it around the chamber to the grooves lining the walls.

"They *are* power conduits," he said aloud.

David lifted the tablet and confirmed Bowen was correct. "But fed on what?"

Outside, the storm had broken, and the clouds were thinning. The light from numerous stars now reached past the cleared plant cover through the open fenestration. The alien ship was recharging on that glow.

"Dad, you said something. It sounded like 'Khamen—'"

"*Duhl*," Bowen said. "The Gardeners."

Bowen turned back to the metal chair.

The machinery set before it shimmered with a dull blue nimbus.

"I spoke with them," he said. "The Ret—the *Khamanduhl*. I think the system operates on a form of telepathy...and that it's interactive!"

Chapter Twenty-two

An artificial intelligence, or the lingering mind of the dead Gardener contained within the system, Bowen reasoned. Maybe it was equal parts both. The identity didn't matter so much as the result.

David passed the tablet over his father's face. He'd called up the biometric panel application and waited for the scan to complete.

"According to mom's last exam of you, everything's identical apart from your leg injury," David said. "I don't read any damage from your interaction with the Khamanduhl machine."

Bowen took a heavy swallow and found that his mouth had gone uncomfortably dry. "Very well then. Let's make this official."

He shuffled toward the chair, but David stopped him. "Dad, may I?"

Bowen shifted his weight onto his good leg. "David?"

"The risks are minimal, according to all data. I'd welcome the chance to talk with them."

Bowen considered the request. David's expression, his face lit by the vague glow emanating from the star-charged instruments, swayed him. "All right, but remember that we need answers about what happened here—and what *is* happening."

"I'll stick to what we discussed."

Bowen nodded. David handed over the tablet and then took to the seat. The same trance-like state that had seduced Bowen quickly embraced David. He found himself adrift in towering purple clouds.

The plumes, David thought.

Through their dense curtains, the dead alien mother ship appeared.

"We are Gardeners," said the androgynous voice.

The greeting was exactly as his father described. No doubt, a standard welcome programmed into the system.

"Tell me what happened to you," David interjected.

An instant later, he was spiraling through a miasma of colored light, falling and being ripped apart.

The black hole!

He heard their screams—twenty-three Khamanduhl trapped in the singularity's hunger and left with no other option than to follow it through to whatever reality waited on the other side.

The Khamanduhl mother ship emerged, but it was damaged, its captain injured. The nearest planet was a barren rock, lifeless and inhospitable. They set out in search of other—

"Wait. The planet," David said.

His view of the gas plumes far beyond Treasure Island shifted, and he found himself facing down from high orbit. Only this version was far removed from the blue world David presently occupied. Its atmosphere roiled with sulfur-colored clouds. The glimpses of the surface visible through the toxic cover showed unforgiving stone terrain pocked with impact craters. It was not the blue planet that the *Altares* mission had come upon.

"An unwelcoming sphere, far from the life-rich soil of Khamanduhl. But with systems failing, our captain succumbed to injuries and gone to Hellennia's Garden, we were left with no other choice."

He returned to the plumes long enough to see the three escape craft drop out of the mother ship's lowest deck. The parent ship went dark. The flotilla of smaller ships turned toward Treasure Island, as it was in that time.

"Others had encountered the planet before us—beings also unfortunate to have been caught in the thirsty grip of the singularity. We detected the remains of seven other space-faring races."

"Seven?"

"One had gone so far as to set in place a complex to alter the planet's nature, to refine its atmosphere and make it breathable. To bring this world to life."

"Terraform it," David said.

The system paused. David sensed it thinking. "To *Khamanduhlform* it, yes. I understand the meaning."

"What became of the First Race?"

"They went extinct before they were able to complete the planet's transformation complex. And, according to our findings, they were the *third* in order of arrival."

His view zoomed in on the planet, and lower to the abandoned city complex. In this capture by the Khamanduhl computer system, the city stood upright and gleamed against the poisonous atmosphere.

"Our new mission was to complete what they began—to transform this world into our new home. A new Khamanduhl. But we were few in number, and the task was monumental."

A series of numerical symbols appeared in one corner of the image. David's mind, linked to the system, translated them as totaling twenty-two.

"We dispatched remote service units to interact with and repair the complex—"

They were outside, looking down at dozens of Ret mech as they streamed toward the city.

"But in their interactions with that other race's technology, they were altered, grew singular in their mission to change the planet for the needs of their creators. But they forgot about us in the process as having created them, for they were now the children of two races. Forgot all save the need to complete the task, at any cost."

The city churned, sucking down toxic atmosphere and releasing purified air. Through a succession of time-lapsed images, the sky transformed to blue. The number twenty-two counted down to one.

"I was the youngest to serve Hellennia, whose garden awaits us in the afterlife. And true to my promise, I guarded the sacred seeds, until the soil of this world welcomed them."

David stood outside with the last of the Khamanduhl crewmembers, watching as the aged alien lovingly drew back the soil and planted a single Iodi seed. Time lapsed once more, through a rainstorm that soaked the crater's heart. The lapse steadied. David looked to see the narrator moving away, toward the alien escape craft where he would die. Around him were numerous graves dug into the dusty soil. But directly beneath where David stood, a single red shoot had broken through the ground.

"Hybrid," Jane said. "Their technology

blended into that of the First Race. Or Third."

"They never intended their devices to be this aggressive," David said. He drew in a deep breath and then just as deeply expelled it. "I saw it. The entire history of this planet after they arrived here. Its transformation from a sterile rock to a living, breathing world. It was amazing!"

"So they're all gone?" Bowen asked.

David nodded. "All that's left of their work here are the flowers and the machines."

"It's the latter that concern me," Bowen said. "David, can we disable any remaining Ret mech from this system?"

"I'm not sure. After they altered with the Third Race's technology, the Gardeners seemed to lose control of them."

"Then can we use that interface to contact *Altares*?"

David returned to the seat. "I'm on it, Dad."

The blast came down from orbit, from an alien ship circling the planet, source of the ground invasion forces. Enemies were here to steal the results of their tireless labor.

Systems long dormant activated, drawing power from starlight. The unit in charge of Khamanduhl affairs sent out the edict: marshal and fight for home soil!

Automated mech woke in the depths of

the silent complex that had transformed the planet from a barren wasteland to a second chance. Some were beyond answering the call. Others began to move, only to malfunction after so long being deactivated and powered down. A good number streamed into the tunnels and dug new ones.

And, deep beneath the ocean's surface, two of the Khamanduhl spacecraft identical to the one where the last Gardener died activated and readied to neutralize the alien threat soaring in high orbit above the planet.

Shervin exited the elevator, gun drawn. She had committed the layout of *Altares'* upper deck to memory on her one earlier visit here, when the light ship was tethered to Space Station Delta. Crew's Quarters. Monitoring Area beyond. From there, Navigation and Flight Deck, and behind the Navigation Area, the famed Photon Drive chamber, which housed the powerful engines that had led them so far from the mother planet.

She swept the compartment with her boom stick, whose setting had been dialed down to its lowest, enough to stun another human. Shervin understood that she was honoring Commander Forbes' wish, made long ago on Delta Station, to not harm *Altares'* crew—especially his favorite.

"Anna Bowen, I need you to show

yourself and release the portside hangar," Shervin called out.

No one answered. Weapon raised, she approached the arch leading into Navigation. Anna Bowen sat at the chart table, studying the screen. She wasn't armed. Shervin smiled. She approached.

"It's Jim Forbes' favorite plaything," Shervin said. "Time for you to unlock that Kite."

She moved to nudge Anna's shoulder with the gun's muzzle. The boom stick passed through, and then the image of Anna crackled out.

A hologram, Shervin thought.

"I'm Tom Bowen's wife," the real Anna Bowen said.

She was in the Drive unit, Shervin realized, before the unmistakable cold point of a boom stick pressed between her shoulders.

"And you don't give orders on Harry Masters' ship."

Chapter Twenty-three

"I have to give it up to you, Anna," Shervin said. "I understand why Forbes found you so fascinating."

Anna reached for the woman's weapon and pulled it from her grasp. "Stop saying his name."

Shervin turned around. Anna retrained her boom stick. The woman raised her hands in surrender. "You could see it in his eyes whenever the subject of you came up."

"It doesn't matter," Anna said. "It was a long time ago."

"You're right. What does matter is that you allow my team to complete its mission. We must head down to that planet, so I'm going to need you to unlock the hangar."

"No," Anna said. "Our team on the ground needs to be extracted. That Kite's our only chance."

Her adversary's smile dropped. "It's far more important that we complete our purpose here."

"You say," Anna fired back. "As far as I'm concerned, you're all criminals that hopped a ride aboard this ship under a cloud of deception."

"The Space Authority is just as guilty. They took Earth Authority fund concessions and sanctioned our being here, in spite of how the situation looks."

The sound of the elevator in motion teased Anna's ear. She took a step back, her aim still on the other woman. "Order them to stand down."

"Or what? You'll shoot me?"

Anna nodded.

"And risk hitting some of your precious equipment, or one of those space windows?"

Anna responded with a cold smile. "I won't miss. Tell them you surrender."

The elevator doors opened. The procession was complete—all three of the interlopers and Masters, his hands raised.

"It looks like we have a stalemate, Shervin," Masters said.

The woman huffed out a breath. "I don't think so. We outnumber you two-to-one."

Silence fell over the Navigation Area.

The two sides faced off, with guns drawn.

Systems long dormant powered up, fueled by starlight and a form of fury expressed through ancient mech and the perception that their silent planet was being invaded.

The first craft broke the ocean's surface and headed across the water. The second Khamanduhl escape ship followed. Fenestrations on both ships released, and out scrambled the machines. The mech took positions across each of the crafts' outer hulls and trained their weapons skyward, at the vessel far overhead, identified by its running lights.

A single mech detached and dropped down to the water. Though two of its electronic eyes were shattered, it navigated its way to shore, and from there turned in the direction of the invaders' landing team, which was holed up in the most sacred of Khamanduhl shrines.

Then, the two spacecraft rose higher and readied for battle.

An alarm bell shattered the tense standoff between members of the Space Authority and Earth Authority.

"Proximity Alert," said Anna.

"What does that mean?"

Masters lowered his arms and brushed away from the tall man and other two Earth Authority soldiers holding him hostage. "It means we've got company."

"Your other Kite?" asked Shervin.

Anna said, "No, the Rets destroyed it with their machines. Tom, David, and Jane survived but they're still down there."

Masters absorbed the information. "Then it has to be something hostile. Space debris, or...Anna."

She maintained her aim on Shervin for another second before lowering her boom stick and hastening over to the wall of computers. A quick scan confirmed it. "Two contacts rising quickly from the surface on an intercept course. Scans match the other Ret escape craft where the ground team is sheltered."

"Can you get a visual lock?"

She did, and projected the view from *Altares'* cameras onto the Navigation Area's screens. The image showed a close up of the nearest vessel, its surface crawling with Ret mech armed and ready to fire.

"They'll reach the outer edge of the planet's atmosphere in twenty seconds," Anna said.

Masters spun back to face Shervin. "They're coming to end both of our missions. Are you willing to join us and fight on the same side, or will you do things the way they've always been done before? Because that way, we all lose!"

Shervin met Masters' gaze. "Lower your weapons," she ordered to her team. "We've got a light ship to defend!"

Masters hopped into the pilot's chair. Anna took Jane's seat and called up the forward laser controls on her instruments.

"Two against one doesn't seem fair," Masters said while inputting the new flight path.

"Not when they're up against *Altares*," Anna said. "I pity them."

Masters smiled. "Shervin, can you handle the aft laser cannon?"

"Of course I can," she answered. And then she added, "*Captain*."

Masters broke orbit, sending *Altares* into a charge that increased the rapidly waning distance between them and the Ret vessels. The light ship surged away from Treasure Island's night side and toward the line of daylight. The planet's sun pulled over the curve of the planet, blinding in its intensity. Masters hoped the glare would work in their favor.

At their six, the pair of alien pursuers split. Anna tracked them. "They're flanking us, coming in fast from Orbital Reference Points two-eleven and six-thirteen."

"Get ready, Shervin."

"Already there, Captain Masters."

"Hold on," Masters called out.

He kicked in *Altares*' forward steering rockets at port and the aft-starboard units. The light ship rolled out of her trim course. Gravity attempted to toss bodies from seats, and sent every loose object in the ship flying. But the violent jolt also lined them up perfectly so that both laser cannons were aligned with the dealers of certain death streaking to flank them.

"Now, Anna—fire! You, too, Shervin.

The forward cannon locked onto its target. Anna thumbed the firing button. *Altares* trembled as the first of two powerful beams surged out of the cannon housed in the directional antenna. Less than a second later, the aft cannon responded. Dual beams of powerful green energy lashed out, striking the alien craft. Twin explosions blazed above the planet, miniature suns there one moment, gone the next.

Shervin appeared at the arch between the Navigation Area and the Flight Deck. "And now what, Captain Masters?"

"Now, we bring our people home."

Confusion threatened to draw David out of the trance. The sky above their position no longer showed the reassuring lights cast by *Altares*.

"They're not up there," he said.

The fugue broke and he found himself seated on the alien chair, in a dark broken only by the vague glow of Khamanduhl instruments.

"David, what do you mean?" asked Bowen.

"The light ship," David said. "*Altares* isn't up there."

Steeling himself, Bowen trudged out of the control room and through the vestibule, to the fenestration. At the open hatch, he searched the sky. True to David's words, *Altares* was no longer visible in the night sky.

Jane moved beside him. "Where did they go?"

Bowen slowly shook his head. That no one had appeared in Kite 2 to extract them from the planet's surface was troubling enough, but now this? A low breeze gossiped through the flower fields, sweet and hypnotic, but also lonely. He thought of the last Gardener, all alone on the planet's surface, knowing he would die, and holding on until he'd fulfilled his mission. A sad, sinking emotion formed in his stomach. What if they were stranded because *Altares* was gone?

"Anna," he whispered.

David appeared behind them in the vestibule. "Dad, we have a problem."

Only one? thought Bowen. He pulled his eyes down from the night sky. "What is it, David?"

"I went into the system for another look, to see if I could locate *Altares*."

"And?"

David shook his head. "But the system picked up a single contact, moving toward us from the direction of the seashore. I think it's another of their armed mech."

Invisible ice formed over Bowen's flesh.

"How close?"

"It's moving in rapidly, should be here in less than one minute."

"Can you close this outer airlock?" Bowen asked.

"I can try," David said, and hurried back inside.

Bowen faced Jane. "We'll set up a line of defense inside. Come on."

They turned and started through the craft's inner airlock. Bowen felt the ground shake an instant before the crash of rocks splitting apart and the cascade of earth from the direction of the crater wall. He looked over his shoulder and saw the Ret mech surging toward them, its two functioning eyes aglow in the darkness.

Chapter Twenty-four

Bowen raised his rifle and fired. A pulse of vibrant white light raced out and struck the Ret mech. Thunder boomed across the canyon. The impact knocked his opponent onto its spine. The Ret device recovered, righted.

"David, get that airlock closed!" Bowen called.

The Ret mech reared up and took aim. Bowen fired again, striking the machine's familiar face. The gun's report echoed across the crater, striking his ears louder than expected. Too loud.

Bowen tracked the source of thunder up, into the sky. Lights surged over the crater wall—it was a Kite! A figure leaned out through the open airlock, rifle drawing a bead on the Ret mech.

Bowen took aim. Jane appeared beside

him and followed suit. All three opened fire as the Ret mech assumed its position. Photon weapons homed in on target. The hostile device held together for another second, rigid atop the graves of its creators, before coming apart in a thunderous explosion of smoke and shrapnel.

The figure leaning out of Kite 2's hatch made a fist and pumped air, then howled in victory.

"Who's that?" Jane asked.

Bowen shook his head. The Kite veered over them and moved into position to land. Bowen looked higher. The light ship *Altares* was over their heads once more, the brightest star in the night sky.

"A second crew?" Bowen asked.

Anna finished dressing his wound. "Both the Earth Authority and the Space Authority sanctioned their presence aboard *Altares*," Anna said. "They were meant as a sort of heritage seed bank, if you will. They'd awaken if we came upon a habitable planet, one ideal for colonization and second chances."

Bowen watched as the four Earth Authority soldiers removed their equipment from the Kite's passenger section. "Not much of a second chance, the four of them on this wide, empty world."

Anna followed his gaze over to the Kite. "What you're looking at is only the beginning,

Tom. Do you see those machines?" Bowen nodded. "Genetic scramblers and portable power units. Contained within those systems are an entire eco-system from basic plant life to pollinating insects, all the way up to colonists selected for the project, an entire catalogue of Earth life reduced to microcosm, in search of a new home. They've found it here, thanks to the Gardeners."

"A new Earth?" Bowen sighed.

"Our second chance."

Their eyes met, and he sensed there was more to her statement than the already immense scope of what would soon begin on the silent blue planet so far from Earth.

"Here's to second chances," Bowen said, and drew Anna into a hug. "I love you, sweetheart."

"And I love you, Tom," Anna said.

"You're sure that was the last of them?" Tasser asked.

David nodded. "I've interacted twice with the Khamanduhl computer system—no more active units register. You'll be able to learn all they knew in this place."

David picked up the tablet.

"And I downloaded a copy to take back with us to *Altares*. Treasure Island certainly lived up to its name."

"Treasure Island," Shervin said.

Folding her arms, she looked around at the vast scope of the planet. Beyond the crater wall, blue ocean glittered beneath bluer skies, leading to illusions about where one ended and the other began.

"What's in a name, right?" Masters asked.

"In this case, everything," said Shervin.

She knelt down, raked her fingers through the soil, and closed her hand around the grains. Tears invaded her eyes.

"Shervin?" Masters asked.

Shervin stood. "We made it. We fulfilled the dream of the Authority's Daughter Initiative."

"*Daughter*," Masters parroted.

"You're standing on Daughter Earth, Captain Masters," Shervin said. "And this time, we promise to get it right."

"Are you sure you don't want to stay, to join us?" Shervin asked.

Masters looked at his crew, all standing in the radiant glow of Daughter Earth's sun. Jane shook her head. Turning back, he said, "We took a vote. Your mission objective has been reached, but ours is still in progress. *Altares* has a long way yet to go."

"I understand, Captain."

Shervin saluted. The three other Earth Authority soldiers did the same.

"Goodbye, and good luck," Masters said.

The two sides shook hands, said farewells, and separated, *Altares'* crew to the waiting Kite. Masters and Jane assumed the two pilots' seats. Anna, Tom, and David huddled close to one another on the passenger bench.

Masters ran through his checklist. "Ready for takeoff," he said.

Vertical thrusters engaged. The Kite jumped up from the crater floor. Horizontal boosters launched them forward. Masters circled the crater wall twice, waved down at the four figures standing among the fields of sacred flowers, and then turned them toward the sky. Long minutes later, they were back in space, and facing the light ship *Altares*.

Two days later, Masters took to the pilot's chair and reached for the pre-flight checklist. He hesitated.

"Are you certain, Jane?"

Jane sat beside him, dressed in a clean regulation uniform, her pre-flight list nearly completed. "You mean about the planet?"

"Yeah."

Daughter Earth turned beneath them, visible through the Flight Deck's forward-facing space window. "I'm happy they're down there, ready to start over," she said. Jane's face brightened with a smile. "I'm certain, Dad."

Masters reached his right hand over. Jane took it in her left. The connection was brief, just enough for him to know their decision was the right one.

"Tom," Masters called out.

"Yes, Skipper," Bowen answered.

"Have you plotted our course out of this system and on to the next?"

Bowen stood at the navigation computer, which displayed their heading on its monitor. He removed the proper disks and placed them into their trays, in sequence.

"Course plotted. Navigation codes activated, Captain."

The signal came in one minute before their plan to break orbit. Shervin's face appeared on screens in both the Flight Deck and Navigation Area.

"Sure there's nothing more you need from us?" Masters asked.

Shervin shook her head and smiled. "No, *Altares*. But thanks for the lift. Thought you might want to see this before your departure."

The remote camera swung away from Shervin toward a patch of soil desolate save for the sole green sprout that had germinated at its center.

"Goodbye, *Altares*," Shervin said.

The image on the screen snowed over.

"Goodbye, Daughter Earth," said Masters.

"Ten...nine...eight," David counted down from the chart table.

"We're ready to leave orbit," Jane chimed in.

"Three...two...one!"

"Engage chemical rockets," Masters ordered.

Jane answered, "Ignition!"

Altares' chemical rockets erupted, and the light ship charged forward, away from the blue planet. Ahead lay a cluster of crystalline stars swimming in a purple fog.

"*Altares* on course," Bowen said.

Masters nodded. "Here we go. Activating Photon drive. Standby."

The light ship arrowed forward. Then she put on a burst of speed and surged ahead, riding a vibrant white comet's tail, and was gone.

Printed in Poland
by Amazon Fulfillment
Poland Sp. z o.o., Wrocław